JAROSLAV DURYCH
GOD'S RAINBOW

MODERN CZECH CLASSICS

Jaroslav Durych
God's Rainbow

Translated from the Czech by David Short

Afterword by Rajendra A. Chitnis and Jan Linka

Karolinum Press

KAROLINUM PRESS, Ovocný trh 3–5, 116 36 Prague 1, Czech Republic
Karolinum Press is a publishing department of Charles University in Prague
www.karolinum.cz

© Karolinum Press, 2016
Text © Jaroslav Durych – heirs c/o Dilia, 2016
Translation © David Short, 2016
Afterword © Rajendra A. Chitnis and Jan Linka, 2016
Illustrations © Jiří Grus, 2016

Cover and graphic design by Zdeněk Ziegler
Typeset by DTP Karolinum
Printed in the Czech Republic by PBtisk a. s., Příbram
First English edition

ISBN 978-80-246-3291-9 (hb)
ISBN 978-80-246-3322-0 (ebk)

This book was kindly supported by the Ministry of Culture of the Czech Republic.

MINISTRY OF CULTURE
CZECH REPUBLIC

There used to be times when, having been seated on a train for several hours, it would begin to dawn on me what I'd forgotten to bring. Back then it wasn't so serious. If I did leave something behind, I rarely regretted it much, because I usually managed perfectly well without it. But this time I was into the fifth day of my journey when I discovered that I had left behind the most important thing of all, namely my better judgement. That had never happened before. How had it happened now?

Well, happened it had. And to the extent that I was quite calm thinking about it, this was actually no odder than that I might ever have had any better judgement at all and that I might subsequently have left even that at home. Such things can and do happen. When all's said and done, if I had acquired some, it was certainly no thanks to any effort on my part, but due more to my incaution, as may occasionally happen to a fish that snaps at something in murky water only for it to get stuck in its mouth and stay there. Thus I, too, had snapped at something in the stagnant sludge beds of my senses, having not the slightest inkling what it might be, and there it was. I'm sure I was no happier about it than the fish about the hook in its mouth, or a dancing bear about the ring in its nose, and I certainly have no recollection of how and from what I recognised that the disagreeable thing that caused me moments of anguish did have a value. Later, though, it brought me occasional gratification. I savoured it, licking and turning it in the wound, and then we grew so accustomed to each other that it stopped aching and pricking and pinching until finally, without my even noticing it, it worked itself loose from the wound and almost fell to the ground at my feet. So I learned how to fix it in and take it out like a gypsy girl's earring, sometimes showing it off in all its lustre, sometimes hiding it as a philandering husband hides his wedding ring. After all, it's not always best judged to exhibit one's better judgement. And that's exactly how I could have happened to leave it at home.

As noted, I only spotted this unfortunate oversight on the fifth day, and not because I'd started to hanker after it. It dawned on me that it was missing in the way I might miss something that isn't particularly essential, but which I'm used to having on me more from habit; I hardly need say that it doesn't weigh much. And yet I was perturbed. Should I have gone back for it?

Certainly not! From the very outset, that journey was evidence enough that the very idea of it had arisen in defiance of the principles of sound judgement. They wouldn't have got along together. So?

There are journeys and journeys. And this was a special one. No one had forced me to undertake it. No one had imposed it on me as a penance. I had sought no one's advice about it and I would not have been deflected from undertaking it by either warnings from friends, or by the dangers and discomforts without which it couldn't have taken place. I had meant to decide on my actual destination only once I was on the way, having selected a region that was little known and even less accessible.

But what was I after?

Well, the choice was mine, wasn't it? To seek seclusion, oblivion and much needed repose, to nurse body and soul and ponder on death and the life to come, as doubtless befits one of my years. But if that were all! Doubtless I might even have seen and admired myself in the mirror of perfection, for therein resides the culmination of all the most precious distractions, and who can resist the urge to have their impeccable charms revealed? Not I for one. Oh, I have seen myself already! Look, there I am! How refined I'm becoming! How I'm getting the better of temptation, of myself, of the world. I'm sure I might have drooled in anticipation. And rightly so. No one who hasn't tried it can believe what it must be like to worship one's own puerility.

However, all that would have been foolish and risible. After all, I could easily have done any of it at home, and it would have been more sensible and above all more genuine. If the point was to rectify my failings, why not go about it at the place where I had committed the offenses? Why escape to some secluded place? Surely that is only permitted when one is being tantalised by a woman, and I am pretty sure that by that age I was being tantalised by none.

But it was worse than that. During those hapless years when I'd looked penury in the face, all the lures of perfection were nothing short of repugnant, and what drove me to embark upon such a strange journey was an impious self-pity, which had grown toxic with my advancing years, and a blasphemous contumacy. And that had often left me feeling apprehensive, because I couldn't trust the living, and I would have been ashamed of myself before the dead. Too late now though! I was on my way.

Oh, old age, you miserable thing! How happily do you descend from your heights to the pit where the carcasses of vain dreams and desires lie interred! How gladly you go back to places you should not!

And why? Is it really so unbearable for the time spent awaiting death to be protracted, or is death unworthy of being awaited with greater patience than one's wedding night? Why are you so sold on it? Where do you think you're going, having donned a ridiculous mask of obduracy, as if, after a thousand days' fasting and a thousand days' praying, you meant to blaspheme mortally? That kind of defiance will gain you nothing. Or are you still impelled to have a good weep over the phantoms of your unaccomplished sins? Do you wish to stir them up like a swarm of rabid flies and wait to see yourself go mad?

The people whom I met and talked to doubtless thought that I was insane, being incapable of concealing how sorry they felt for me. But seeing that I was in earnest, and being quite well-meaning, they tried to smooth my troublesome passage, assisting me by word or deed, and thus I reached the furthermost little town to which I could travel, with all my luggage, by some means of transport or other, thence to trudge onwards on foot. The sight of me would certainly have made a cat laugh. Look, a man well into his sixties, unaccustomed to physical exertion and not in the best of health, heading out, stick in hand and a heavy rucksack on his back, for some place where even crows would croak themselves to death, but where he wishes to live alone, quite alone, although he is generally clueless and woefully lacking in experience.

But there I was, on the way. I'd left my larger items of luggage with some kindly folk in the town and kept with me just enough to see me through ten days or so, so at first the going was fairly good. Then it got harder. Not so much on the shoulders, or on the lower back. It was hardest on the eyes, then on the mouth and the ears.

I grew used to the sight of spellbound settlements that were more like the funerary assembly points of lost souls than places where living beings had dwelt, and to the sight of abandoned and weed-infested fields over which not even crows could be bothered to fly, and every step I took created an echo like an unremitting call to pray for the departed, or like one unending and painful litany. There weren't many houses tumbling down or already in ruins, but that only made everything all the gloomier. Doors ajar, and behind them a silent, frightful darkness. Plant pots on window ledges, the plants in them withered brown. Instead of curtains cobwebs dangled. Oh, those cobwebs! Scary, and they knew it! I was certain that the spiders that had spun them had also dried up with fright. And there were uprooted fences, stakes with no goats attached to them, kennels without dogs, fruit trees that no one harvested, and the gloomily spectacular thickets of nettles and sundry weeds with which Nature had replaced human life, or rather wiped out all trace of it. And yet it was still not entirely forlorn. In the distance at least there was still smoke to be observed rising from a chimney. And here and there the imprints of wheels, and even of hooves and boots, had not yet been obliterated. There were still people here who had survived the devastation.

All around on the hilltops and steep scarps forests daydreamed, living their own lives, breathing their own breath and gloomy with their own, not in the least human, gloominess. There had been times when I'd found that alluring. Times! Times past! But this time things were quite different. Now I no longer needed to seek refuge in them, or solitude, a place to hide from anything that reminded me, however remotely, that there were people in the world. Their abodes had ceased to be offensively repellent and characteristically sordid and had taken on a conciliatory, cadaverous beauty and a sombre magnificence. A deathly hush reigned in majesty over all, death was everywhere, every house was like a tomb, everything was gaping into eternity. The forests that used to seem so pure and noble and beautiful, ah, how might they ever compare now to the purity, nobility and beauty of this ineffable silence of devastation and death! The most desperate cry of a bird strangulated in the direst spot was as nothing compared to the creaking of a gate hanging off its hinges. The beauty of scudding clouds seemed barely of note until reflected in the black, lifeless and sightless panes of the low-set windows.

The breath of the loveliest of Indian summers acquired its true sweetness only when mixed with the odour of advanced decomposition and decay, and the eye was lured less by the showy wings of belated butterflies than by the languid lumbering of carrion-seeking blowflies. And the best spot to take one's ease was not on the untouched moss or amid the heather, but on the thresholds of the abandoned and bygone cottages and in the shade of the contorted lindens whose ageing away in the graveyards had passed unperceived.

I would have liked to walk by as slowly as possible. I would have liked to pause at every threshold. I would have liked to carry on walking until deep into the night, maybe until God's break of the day. Oh, could there be anything more awesome than to gaze into the darkness behind the black and lifeless panes of the low-set windows against which I pressed my forehead and my mouth and nose?

Surely it was inconceivable that nothing would look out from behind them ever again. I kept expecting that those dead and motionless cobwebs would, after all, suddenly part and that through them at least the spectre of a tormented visage would show itself, whether human or ophidian, and that it, from its side, would also press against the glass, whether to frame a kiss, or a snakebite, or any other token that would not, either then or later, be made real unless our motion-lessly appressed and benumbed lips broke through the glass that separated us like death or a curse. And the darkness behind those half-open doors! How it threw one off-balance! The drumming in one's ears and the stabbing sensation in one's brow! How terrifying it was, how stupefying, and how it coaxed one to one's knees to await death!

My advancing years had begun to give notice of their demands. I hadn't covered much ground, but had had nothing to eat or drink since the morning because the awe inspired by these afflicted places would not have permitted it. And then when the sun began to dip more alarmingly towards the earth and my mind, after a whole day spent meandering through these deserted places, started clouding with a peculiar, suffocating sorrowfulness, it began to dawn that I ought really to proceed with all haste to my destination and there, while it was still light, seek out somewhere fitting to spend the night.

I noticed that the road ahead twisted and turned before arching broadly towards a forest that could be reached in a much straighter line by a steep, but wide sunken track, and it struck me that it would be better if I took a short cut along this track.

If I were indeed to take this short cut, I would, unless I were to walk backwards, have to turn my back on all these spectral places. I felt rather awkward about that. It was as if I would be turning my back on an uncanny graveyard with ravaged and empty graves, in which lay neither coffin nor corpse, as if from some particular date no one had been permitted to die and as if the dying had had, by some incomprehensible device, to bear their bodies away straight to the Other Side. But fatigue was adding to the instability of my mind, whose attention was now engaged by the forest as a welcome change.

Its trees were quite young and at first it seemed quite an ordinary forest. But then it began to exude a balmy scent. And now I was faint and the balm was stupefying. At first only my hearing went berserk, as in the midst of an infinite, ponderous silence, then my sight started playing games and soon I was beset by various imaginings in the face of which I would, on any other occasion, have begun to tremble, but this time I desired that they would not leave me and perhaps take me with them all the way to perdition. They were akin to those visions of a felicity that has been devoured by time or veiled over by death. But common sense told me that I was acting like a dog who runs ahead and hasn't noticed that he's dragging a chain as well. But try arguing with someone who doesn't know what he wants!

So I walked on and on until I entered a glade, where, on one side, stood some strangely illuminated and seemingly bewitched and spellbound spruces, across whose silent and dreamy rooftops the light danced like surges of pinkish and bluish waves hurrying off for a romp in the adjacent darkness. And I saw the sky and the clouds, more alone than I had ever been myself, and I felt sad and something whispered suggestively:

That's her! There! Can't you see?

But all I could see was a jay flying, or rather the fleeting shadow of it, more reminiscent of a distressed bat. Then the surges of pinkish and bluish waves seemed to want to laugh at something. And maybe they did laugh. Though my keyed-up hearing perceived no more than the mournful rasp of the old jay and the tweeting of its young. Only the treacherous sorrow in the dark recesses of my soul told me:

Just look! Don't you recognise her? The sublime glitter on the spruce trees! The airiness! The stoop of the branches! Can you really not remember her dress, or her face, or how she stood as she looked down, clinging to the golden gate of God's rainbow, down into your boyhood dreams.

The silent surges of pinkish and bluish waves rolled on. Overhead, the rooftops of the spruces turned grey, ahead of me the forest thinned and all around me stood tall trees that admitted a magical light in wide, slanting and iridescent stripes, waiting for beings invisible to my tired eyes to suspend a canopy from them and for that most beautiful one to appear beneath the canopy, she who had looked down, clinging to the golden gate of God's rainbow, down into my boyhood dreams. And now I was approaching those strips of light that were like columns supporting the weight of both sun and rainbow, and something prompted me to leave the path and draw near, touch them and lean against them and wait. Maybe she will come. And I might have walked on, but the recollection of years bemourned and buried detained me. I told myself:

Do you even know if she's alive? And if she isn't dead, she has certainly so aged that nothing would trouble us so grievously as my having not come before this.

But the voice replied:

Are you not afraid to say it? And if she were, as you say, dead, should you now not be chasing after her and seeking and kissing that grave, or, more likely, digging with fingers, elbows and arms and head all the way

down to her? Just hurry along and tarry not! It's now, or never!

Well, it sounded encouraging. I was completely alone and I could have done even the most ridiculously silly things. And yet I said to myself:

And where am I supposed to be going?

The voice replied at once:

You are seeking a vision of beauty, you are seeking a vision of immortality, and you ask such a question? Just go on! Just keep looking down, up! Don't go looking for excuses and be on your mettle! Ask the squirrels if they know anything about her hiding place! Or, perhaps better, the jays. They can fly around the forest and see everything –

I walked on. The path narrowed, passing between two rows of spruces. Their branches pressed fondly into the grass, trying my poor senses with the odd chimera of an image that refused to take shape, but so acted upon me that tears welled up in my eyes. I quickened my step, believing that it would pass. And the shadows slowly lengthened and erased the glitter and glint of the sunlight. But suddenly – What's this?

To one side, above the spruce trees, a golden, piercing light gleamed. It was motionless, it did not fade and it quite dazzled me. I raised my eyes, desirous to know anyway what it was. I was disappointed, but also cheered, for I descried in the distance one tall spruce which held, in the embrace of its most winsome, its highest branches, a large cone. A radiance shot forth from it as from a golden onion dome adorning a church spire. My heart jumped, it was as if the cone knew everything and was itself pointing whither and which way I should go. And I was so confounded that I tripped, failing to watch the way beneath my feet, and if I had –

I almost jumped out of my skin. Yes, it was a viper. And a huge one at that! I pulled up short, at a distance of not quite two paces from it, but it didn't even move. It was disgustingly brown and doubtless old and over-bearing and self-assured, for it lay there peacefully and wound into a coil right there in the middle of the track. And I might well have been surprised at happening right then – at the autumn equinox, at a time with the days shortening and a fairly raw coldness rising from the earth – upon a viper of all things. But for now I was still dazzled by that shining cone and the memory of a girl, looking down, clinging to the gate of a heav-enly rainbow, down into my boyhood dreams, and I stood there and stared and choked back my anger at that stupid cone, and if I could, I would have knocked it down. But now there was this viper preventing me. What now? Jump on it and trample it to death? That struck me as trickier than it is in reality. Beat it to death with my stick? If that failed, I would look silly. The ground was grassy, lumpy and damp and soft. But what would I do if I succeeded? Would there be any point to it? It would lie there and haunt me. That I couldn't stand. I'd have to come back and bury it. Would there be any point in so doing? No, there wouldn't. In the middle of sleepless nights it would scare me with its eyes overflowing with dark malevolence and ignobility and an infernal sorrowfulness. If I were to destroy it as I needed, I would surely have to pick it up, tear it in two and swallow it piecemeal, for it reminded me all too clearly of my own soul. So what then?

The oblique rays of the sun reflected spectrally off the beastly thing, which was exposing its monstrous body to their final glimmer. The shadows were almost upon it. Maybe that was all it had taken to make it coil up. It hadn't wanted to go into hiding just yet. So I waited, impatient for the cold to set it shivering. But I did feel sad.

That, then, was how I was received by that enchanted place, that wistful and heavenly forest! The first to welcome me was a viper. And that was right now, just as the curse was lifted from the earth and the sky shone bright with God's rainbow. But that probably didn't apply to this spot. This spot had perhaps been left to the mercy of serpents. Yet it was to this spot that my spirit had led me!

But suddenly the truth dawned and my heart skipped. Wherein lay the connection between the insidious glitter of that shining cone and this hideous snake? What if the snake was showing me something, whatever that might be? If it was impeding my weary steps, surely it must be guarding paradise.

It had to be stirred, but calmly and pacifically and as sweetly as possible. It must not take offense. But what was I to say to it?

"You sod, you," I addressed it, "are you alive? So what about it?"

Well, that was certainly no testimony to any shrewdness on my part. I understood as much only after the mistake was made and I felt in every joint that my punishment would be swift. So I stood and waited.

At first, nothing. My husky voice seemed merely to course through its body like a bluish shadow. Then its listless, wrinkled head rose, only to drop back to where it had been. Then the slits of its wicked eyes slowly opened half-way, then closed again. And that was all. It was sleepy. It didn't know whether it might be dreaming or what was happening, and it didn't look at me. I was standing behind it and it would have had to turn round slightly. For which it had neither the desire, nor the strength. And my unflattering and facetious way of addressing it must surely have had time to mature inside its flattened head, so it was perhaps right to assume that I was probably some creature more obtuse and vulgar than a dog, if not worse even than a hedgehog.

But suddenly, like some drowsy watchman, it came to and twitched as if slightly bothered. It raised its obscene neck with a head like an unopened water lily bud disgorged from a suddenly dried-up mud-bed and trodden down just for the hell of it, and, blinking obscenely with its evil eyes, it jerked its flattened head first to the right, then back, then to the left. And it was comical, because it didn't turn to face me, though it must have felt my shadow on its body, but I was also taken by how those jerks of the head, while frankly evil, had a measured nobility and gentle grace to them. Such actions can only be those of a creature tenderly in love when, in the bosom of its sweetheart, it is woken by the call of death out of the sweetest of dreams. And suddenly I also recalled that hand, coaxing from the palely shining keys the jerky, boisterous and wistful sounds that subdued all heartache and laughed at tears. And I saw that arm, bared to the elbow, and the cheekily gushing and dying glitter of those jerky sounds as I had witnessed it at the last playing, before the roses faded and the hoarfrost descended –

Right now I would surely have loved to hear those sounds, at least with my eyes. But the viper seemed disinclined to play, and if it did play something, it was inadvertent and of short duration. It froze again in a convulsion of pride and venom, and if it hadn't been lying there in the middle of the path like a snare for a suicide, I might have thought that it was all a dream.

I know not how I then realised that it had sunk deep in thought. Obviously, I would have liked to know whether it might not be watching, perhaps through some sliver of glass concealed inside its eye, at least a refracted image either of what I was or of what I wanted to be, or whether I wasn't being mirrored in its scales in a way that made it feel ill, and without my suspecting a thing. But then it stretched out its neck and a strange tension passed visibly through the coils of its body, betraying its intention either to fight or play some dirty trick. I am sure I even trembled and held my breath, but I was already captivated. The first coil rose like a bow stretched taut, then it froze and waited with such dogged determination, as if reluctant to release from its embrace something of which the tongues of men, like vipers' tongues, perhaps may hiss and little more. Then the raised neck slowly extended with its head away from me, not upwards, but completely horizontally, though not in my direction. It could have been a ploy or the prelude to unfurling the remaining coils. The next heavy coil followed rather more laboriously, changing the alignment of the sides and grumpily rebalancing after a sudden temporary hitch, and yet it did regain its balance and slip and slide downwards like faithless

delight abandoning the exhausted. And suddenly, as I watched, I felt my whole body twisting, my ribs and vertebrae creeping and groaning, my lips getting longer and pointier and my nose flattening. And I could see that the whole outstretched, tense part of the snake was floating over something invisible that permeated the air, for though it extended and tensed itself so far out that it could no longer keep its monstrous weavings in balance, it still hadn't touched the ground. And it was all so defiant and evil, as if the viper couldn't bear to contemplate the moment when I would see the embarrassment of its slithering, but supercilious frame. And again it put me in mind of that lovely hand at the last playing –

But not even the viper's powers were unlimited, and that which had held it aloft, whether pride or shame, could barely resist the forces of gravity. Its head started to drop and its neck bent right down to the ground. At that instant, the second and last coil sprang, its head vanished beneath a young spruce branch where it lay pressed to the ground and then, ponderously and with dignity, the rest of its impressive and monstrous body followed the same way. And that was all. Not a leaf wavered and not a shadow in the grass flickered.

Now the path was free and I could walk on. But suddenly something buffeted my ribs so unbearably as if I was meant to bear thenceforth until eternity the dark, zig-zag stripe borne by the viper on my own wretched back. And I felt sad and stood and pondered.

Why did that hideous viper have to go and lie so impertinently in the middle of *my* way? Had it settled there from habit? Had that spot seemed so cosy to it? Ah, I'm sure it was expecting me. I'm sure it was guarding the track. Why did it let me pass? Had I offended it with the coarseness of my language?

At that point I spotted my shadow. The sun now stood low and was making fun of me by elongating the shadow of my nose. It was infuriatingly ludicrous, but seemed no impediment to the shadow. It rose in vanity, stretched out even more and started to laugh.

So what then? Do you feel better? Why did you begin with such irreverence? Do you think you're better than a viper? Surely not since the day you resolved to go playing the hermit. That would be wrong. Are you telling me you've read somewhere about hermits who swear at vipers?

I would have spat on the shadow, but something held me back and I lapsed into reverie. That stupid cone led me to the viper. And why? The hideous viper, I'm sure, knew many things. Who knows if its scales had not mirrored her who had looked down, clinging to the golden gate of God's rainbow, down into my boyhood dreams! And now the viper had disappeared for good and hadn't even given me a hiss –

My wretched shadow propped itself on my stick and began to titter:

And where are you actually going? What vice is pushing you there and what's the allure of the place? Is it perhaps that that wandering spirit, the one that's abandoned its messy and faintly smelly abode in your stupid head and, rather than live with you, has preferred to haul itself off to Sodsville to amuse the demons and crows? And you want to play the hermit? You'd be better off going back.

Now I didn't know whether it was lying, or telling the truth, for it spoke so scathingly that falsehood itself must have blushed with embarrassment. But then I remembered the viper and imagined how amazed it would be were I to have yielded to the spitefulness of my despicable shadow and gone back to where I had left my better judgement. That was the last straw. I looked at my villainous shadow as at a cur and responded:

What would the viper have said?

My villainous shadow stretched out, its immanent schadenfreude urging me to follow it. I might have bewailed my better judgement, mouldering away as it was in my locked flat, but I had to go on. And I kicked wrathfully at my villainous shadow, which was hurrying forward like a woman-fancier after his fancy woman, but I had to go on.

All was quiet. The forest smelled pleasant. And I felt as if the viper was creeping ever behind me, secretly and inaudibly. But should I have felt afraid? Or should I have despised it? What was I holding against it? That it was so old? So wise and circumspect? So loftily repugnant? And I? Let's not waste words on me. How on earth could I compare with it! Or might I have been anxious solely because it had so humiliated me by its own hideous perfection? But what if it were to slither in to visit me in the night and seek to bite me.

Never mind! Let it come crawling if it will! And suppose this very day –

I was tired. By now I was tottering slightly. The forest thinned and my eyes, hitherto happy with the shade of the dense growth of spruce, began to be jabbed at by firedust-like sparks shooting from the sinking, lumbering sun. But this didn't last long and as I came out of the forest, I spotted a hollow, now sunk in purple shadows, and the road that I was to descend towards. And something laid a hand on me and I had to stop and take a look all round. And I saw the sky. It was majestic, but horrible as an image of smouldering corpses. And I could see mountains, looking like volcanoes, or the forsaken frontages of part-demolished churches, or abandoned altars or thrones. And I saw the hollow, sunk in purple shadows and an awesome, incomprehensible and insane silence. But however I tried to avoid it, averting my gaze and apprehensive, it was to no avail. To one side, above the hollow, was something that outshone and outgloried even the rays of the setting sun.

I was frozen to the spot. I was in dread of it and it drew me on like a premonition of an unutterable something that happens but once, never to be repeated. And I suddenly felt that I should run towards it and there fall upon my face, and only regretted that my legs were so short and my breath likewise, and I was only afraid lest I miss a fitting moment for death.

So this is what the gleaming spruce cone had been pointing me to. This is why the viper lay in my path, seeking to delay and seduce me. This was then that paradise, possibly certain now and attainable. I just needed to get a grip and go, and if the last ounces of my powers abandoned me, to drop my rucksack and cast aside my stick, get down on all fours, roll over and start to crawl, thrusting myself forward like a snake using all my ribs and ultimately my chin and my vainglorious nose. And I descended to the road, close to a hamlet that was disappearing in the mute shadows of evening, and I was tramping over dust, white, sorry dust, un-

tainted by a single human or animal footprint, until I spotted a point from which a long flight of steps rose up to the side, shaded by two rows of linden trees. And I saw a cemetery and all manner of interesting things, but didn't linger there. Upwards!

I thought I was going to drop down and die. But I had to keep going, even if that meant crawling, towards that gleaming magnificence which blissfully surpassed the heads of the truncated lindens with its graceful tower. It had another tower besides, but that was unfinished and had a rowan growing out of its levelled-off stub. And this was a truly regal spot that attracted all the rays of the sun and the envy of the mountains, and the entire structure floated in the dazzling, ethereal glare like a revelation of the partly open gateway to Heaven.

I tottered, but more with joy and faintness, and walked on, albeit with heavy tread, yet with as light a heart as if this paradise were waiting for me alone. I cannot say if I was moved to pray. I gave it no thought and understood no more than that I had to crawl there on all fours, catching the edges of the steps with my chin, or nose even, and only at the top would I be able to rest, fall face to the ground and eat the dust.

But I wasn't vanquished and did duly reach the door. Well, what should I have expected? It was closed. Undaunted and with my customary abandon I tried the handle, mindless of what would come next. To my great surprise and horror, the door almost flew off its hinges inwards, taking me with it.

I doffed my cap, crossed myself, closed the door behind me and dropped to my knees. I was greeted by a leaden, musty darkness and I began to look for the altar, but I could see nothing but blackened cobwebs, snagged and swaying and lit by a strip of dim, deflected light. There was no sanctuary lamp visible. Perhaps it had gone out.

I saw circles before my eyes and began to feel that death was at my back. Ah well! At least I was on my knees. But I felt sad. I hadn't imagined it like this. I would have happily fallen to the ground and kissed it, but something was holding me back. But then I could see nothing except the blackened cobwebs in the faint light and all round them darkness. But then I could hear nothing but the pounding of my worn and heavy heart, answered from all sides by nought but the sullen silence. On the other hand, I did sense the heavy, stifling stench that was rising in intensity and bitterness as a warning from the profanatory and unclean darkness in which the church was cloaked.

I began to consider going back outside and sitting beside the main door, believing that if I had to die, then preferably in the fresh air. Then because I am naturally stubborn, I decided otherwise. I would walk through the dark as through a devils' hideaway and take a look at the desecration that this enchanted church held within it. I took one step, my eyes fixed on the ground to avoid tripping up, then a second and a third, when at the next step I froze with fright.

Something seemed to be slithering across the dead flagstones towards me. What was it? A spectre of derangement? An unclean illusion? Then at once the thing slithering towards me across the floor froze likewise. And I felt faint and my heart kept skipping. Yet I would have dearly liked to know whether the spectre of derangement was the unclean thing that had become motionless before me, or whether it was I myself.

I would have liked to stamp on it, but in the dark I couldn't tell where it ended and where it had crawled out from. And I felt faint and there was a pain in my ears as if I were hearing the laughter of devils. And I seemed to be in an unblessed place, which I would not be leaving alive.

I was convinced that each stone of this abandoned temple was saturated with the stifling miasma. And the timbers! Had not the beams and rafters, the frames of pictures, the grilles, pews, confessionals and altar panels become warped? Had not all the nails and spikes rusted away and all the spiders and flies died? And had I not found myself inside a temple of the seven unclean spirits?

But I was still standing there and holding out, being set on dropping down dead rather than leaving, having gained nothing for my pains. Let the devils mock! Onwards –

But what was that?

Only a sound like a drip falling with a brief echo that faded away in the bowels of the unclean darkness. Yes, it must have been a drip dropping. Surely. It shot through me like a painful spasm. Then silence again. Alone a mysterious and inaudible and unclean laughter shook the black cobwebs.

Then I had an idea: suppose I opened the door. And I would have made a move, but then it struck again, close at hand and enough for the fright to make me see.

Aha! That's it!

I breathed again, having recognised a bier with a black coffin on it. The dripping could only be coming from there. My senile eyes had grown accustomed to the darkness and even made out the inevitable pool on the stone floor. It had dried out round the edges and a viscid ooze dribbled from it in a meandering, faltering trickle such that anyone coming into this unholy obscurity from the full glare of the sun might think that it was crawling and twisting.

Well, I marvelled, recollecting my foolish dream, the oddly lit and enchanted spruces, those floods of pinkish and bluish waves, the glowing cone and the snake on the path. So this is what I was looking for! So this is that tomb, this that dead woman! Yes, now I have everything. So what next?

I went over to the coffin. It was lidded and nailed down. Yet a single touch would surely reduce it to debris along with that which lay rotting within it. But who put it there? What lay encased within it?

I looked about me and thought that invisible beings were also looking down on it, stupefying their enfeebled senses with the bitter cadaverous smell and abstractedly counting the ticking of the drips in lieu of the ticking of a clock. Night could have fallen, given that the rays of deflected, murky light that a moment before had lit up the filthy cobwebs like a profane halo, had faded and died. And now I was alone and began shifting my feet, still uncertain of whether I ought not to remain now in this spot. But suddenly I was shot through by a piercing and paralysing and sarcastic sound like a screeching of glass. I scraped one foot and realised that what had screeched so acerbically was the glass of the sanctuary lamp, which had shattered at its own extinction. And now I felt a touch of such desperate sorrow that I wished most of all to drop down there and die on those shards of glass, which were telling me just how futile were my longings and how trifling my dreams.

So why didn't I? Why did I not drop down?

I was thwarted by a sudden fatigue of the senses and a hissing of the distrust that had hitherto been sleeping in my heart. How, it wanted to know, and from where did I know that this reeking coffin held that very being who looked down, clinging to the gateway of a heavenly rainbow, down into my boyhood dreams? What if it held a man? Or a mangy dog? I should just yank the lid off and reach inside!

That would, I thought, be the most sensible. But in the dark? No, no! There was no hurry now, and if night had come, day too must come. And then?

Something at least. Maybe my pilgrimage did have some unforeseen, but sensible reason. I was to dig a grave, bury a body and cleanse a church. Well, I'd wanted to do a spell of hermitry, and with no effort on my part a task had presented itself, the performance of which demanded considerable effort *and* time, since I still had to lay my hands on at least a pick and spade, and a broom and pail.

My blood was slowly cooling and I could now laugh at my confused dreams and genially nod my clever-clever head. Right! I could now happily find somewhere to spend the night in the nearest convenient house, with a bed even, no matter how shabby, but certainly more comfortable than a stinking puddle and slivers of glass. Right! I turned, reached the dilapidated doorway and, having failed to find the handle, would have begun to curse, if not stamp my foot and hop up and down, for by now I was afraid that I might be stuck there like a badger in a trap – except that I did find it and was almost sent flying by the sudden flood of light and the door itself. All my fatigue passed, my anxiety was behind me and even the sorrow fell silent.

And I came out of the church.

The sun meanwhile was sinking behind the mountains, the shadows in the hollow growing denser and the first stars twinkling overhead like candle flames. Only on the slopes of the abandoned and mournful fields was the light still shining bright, and above the forests the silent floods of pinkish and bluish waves that had reached their goal smouldered still. And as I stood there, contending with the dazzle and the vertigo of feeling faint and maybe even shaking like one already passing out, from the hillsides, ruminating on their limitless dereliction, a gold and rufescent light began to shine intensely as from seven invisible and miraculous gateways and with it blistering sparks of green, purple and pallid blue. And it felt cold and it felt hot, and it wailed and fell silent, and it dragged on and it shook, and the tops of the mountains above rose wistfully like the frontages of long-collapsed churches and the cottages and houses cowered in the half-light like forgotten coffins, and no dog barked, nor did any crows caw, only some wild geese flew high, high above, bearing away with them the last golden glow, and the land below seemed to writhe in terror.

I sat on a step and watched. Behind me was that door that had opened with such ease, within me the exhaustion of my heart, and ahead of me the deserted and spellbound landscape and approaching night. And I sensed many things, but understood nothing, and I had to watch and watch, and when I'd had my fill of watching, I stood up, meaning to go now and seek a bed for the night. Yet I couldn't move from the spot until I'd had another look behind me.

For that way lay the church. Its plasterwork was flaking away and I could see that its lower part was made of stone and the upper of bricks. And as I looked at the stone, I seemed to see there traces of all the vipers who had ever left their sloughed skins on it. But that was nothing, for the frontage of the church floated upwards, making a mockery of all the laws of gravity, like a vision of infinity, and it rose higher and higher until my eyes nearly popped. And the red sky began to fade, the shadows to darken, obscuring even the foot of the church wall, but I was still expecting to hear a voice, whether from the living or the dead, whether of thunder or an earthquake, and suddenly, whether from infinity or from the tombs, the words of an anthem roared forth:

tuba mirum spargens sonum
per sepulcra regionum
coget omnes ante thronum –

Yes, this is how I would imagine both the sense of and the image behind these words of warning. Tombs of beings and landscapes. Tombs of sins and suffering. Tombs of clouds and hills. Tombs of tombs.

But suddenly the image faded, so I walked down to the road, which was so winding that in a few minutes the church vanished from sight like a dream, not to be seen again.

I could have chosen any one of the cottages that I passed. Mostly they weren't even locked up, and many also had the windows open, with the wind blowing the year's first fallen leaves in through them. Apparently they'd been abandoned in haste, for I could see both curtains at the windows and duvets on the beds, and even cloths and crocks on the tables. Were it not for the nettles with which the doorways were overgrown and which were also invading the hallways, and for the blackened cobwebs at the windows and half-open doors, it might have seemed as if the householders were out in the fields and could return at any minute. But weary as I was, I was disinclined to stay here. That could have simply been down to the resolution that I'd

made not to rest that day until I reached the hamlet of which I knew nothing, about which I had asked no one, but which I had chosen as the destination of my crazy expedition. I may also have hoped that at the place that I hoped to reach the ghosts would be more welcoming and the distractions more agreeable.

43

The sky was clear and the waxing moon was shining and with it the smooth and pure-white dust on the road. I might have begun idly dreaming about the sky, the moon, my footprints in the dust and other foolish things, but just then some cottages appeared and I wanted to make a choice of one. Which one, though? Well, there was certainly no need to worry that someone might nose me out without warning, but I still didn't want to be caught out, so I looked for something as far back from the road as possible. But there was nothing standing alone or in a nook somewhere, everything being bordered on both sides. What now? I would have had to start going from house to house, taking a quick sniff round, but that struck me as slightly improper. I paused and cogitated and waited and I might have stood there cogitating until I went barmy if I hadn't suddenly caught the sound of running water.

Ah! Was there ever a sweeter sound? Now I knew what I was seeking and soon I spotted the path to a stream in the shade of two lines of trees, and I went on and my heart sang to that blissful song. I came to a footbridge and crossed it, not looking into the cool darkness that concealed the lips and eyes of the water, and I kept on walking and then I thought I really was asleep and only seeing the fairly large house as in a dream and was unable to decide whether I should enter it or not. Then I saw nothing, though I did manage to close the door and stagger into the kitchen, where I struck a match and saw that it was neither tidy nor untidy, but that there was nothing there to lie on. That quite suited me, for insofar as I wished to play the master of such a big house and command the respect of all its spirits, I needed to seek out a more, if not the most, suitable room.

I scrambled upstairs and almost regretted it at once, because there were two closed doors opposite each other. Which was I to enter? The one on the right? The one on the left? I was saved by my very weakness and weariness. I chose the closer one and, exhaustion having got the better of me, I dropped my rucksack and collapsed onto a chair.

A huge, bright star was peeking in through the half-open window, but my only thought was of which bed I should take, there being two in the room, and standing right next to each other. This would surely have been an insoluble problem, but fortunately for me the two beds were not the same, or if they were, they were at least not in the same state and I was able to guess which of them was deserving of more trust.

The point being, that one of the beds was made up, the other unmade. The made-up one seemed more welcoming and communicative, the unmade one seeming mute and deaf. But the made-up one was not apparently got ready for some guest, since the duvet had been left rather casually across the foot of the bed, the pillow was squashed and the sheet rumpled as if the last person to lie there had had troubled dreams. And I began to wonder.

Who *had* lain there, and where was he now? Was he alive? Might he not pop back for a moment and have a little chat? But possibly he hadn't risen from the bed of his own volition. Possibly they had dragged him from it, hence the rumpled sheet. And might he not be lying in that coffin now, and might it not be my unfathomable task or punishment to concern myself with him as the sole thing that brought me here?

In my state of abstraction I might almost have taken that bed, but something held me back. What if he comes to haunt the place? Which bed will he want if he does come back? Might he take offense that I have occupied his bed, even though it is quite unoccupied?

I made up the other bed, the mute and deaf one, undressed, donned my nightshirt and, quickly crossing myself, lay down at last. And only after I had lain down did I realise that I hadn't closed the window, but lacking the strength to rise again, I pulled the duvet over my ears instead and inhaled something that reminded me of the smell of corpses, lindens in bloom and a good-bye kiss. And I began mulling over those sombre wooden cottages, the forest, the crazy spruce cone and the sleeping viper, the gleaming church with its black coffin, the song of the stream, the desolation of these enchanted places, and the star peeping in through the window, but it wasn't long before I fell asleep and slept, dead to the world.

I slept really soundly for about an hour, and as I began to come to, it took me a while to sort out what my physical senses were telling me from what the departing spirits of my dreams were still mocking me with. Not all my vices and all my virtues were awake yet, only my selfishness and sloth.

First I heard something like a wild burst of clucking of frightened chickens. In the struggle between senile inertia and irresponsibly permitting my imagination to have its way, inertia came out ahead. I had no urge to tax myself with thinking. Is it even fitting for a man who is old and more or less at peace with himself to give thought to the clucking of hens? But my imagination itself would not be brushed off and promptly presented me with sundry sorcerous poultry so that in the space of a few seconds I had scanned whole rows of bogeys rearing their chicken heads from low-set coops. Then came something like the jangling of a chain, the bleating of a goat and the banging of a wicket gate. It was surely nothing that a sensible person need have taken fright at if his mind was not on burglars, and why should it have mattered to me if someone wanted to look in on a chicken or goat? Yet not only the jangling of the chain, but also the bleating of the goat and the banging of the wicket gate were something that the spirits of dreams began rapidly weaving into the bleakest image imaginable of an almost supernatural horror. And so as not to be the lunatic to my imagination, I girded up my loins to haul myself from my stupor and suddenly caught another banging sound and then –

Yes, footsteps.

Then, to my considerable annoyance, I realised that I wasn't lying in the same place as the previous night, where I needn't have cared who was asleep and who was awake. And I began to piece together both where I was and how I'd got there, and suddenly it struck me that something wasn't right.

Maybe the house had been entered by some being that had been the cause of both the hens' clucking and the chain's clanking, the goat's bleating and the gate's banging. Had it only just arrived? Definitely. For when I arrived there hadn't been a soul in sight, whether of hen, goat or any other living thing. But what kind of being must it be to venture this far in the dark and with chickens and a goat?

The longer I mulled, the less I understood. I opened my eyes a chink. The moon was shining. Then it dawned that I could get up and look out of the window. The obstacle to that, however, was my sloth and indolence. So I had to pause for thought. Then I was pleased that my reason had taken charge of my sloth. For it was already too late. The being, if such it even was, was now inside the house, so I would have seen nothing from the window and only chilled my feet to no purpose. My complacency was, however, of only brief duration. For my reason did concede that it could be some being. It could have seemed odd that it had come now and as if to see me. Did it not have plenty of other options closer to the road?

Then my heart suddenly skipped a beat. Had the being perhaps lived here before and had come here for the night, whereas I was only there to haunt the place?

Of course I was unprepared for that and would dearly have liked to beat an immediate retreat. But which way and where to? The window was too high, and if I were to have gone down by the stairs, I should certainly have run into the person. That would have been unfortunate. A cry of terror and the soothing and apologising and explaining – I didn't want that. And up to the loft? I'd be bound to trip over something. It was already dark, after all. So what was I to do?

What came to my aid at this point was my geriatric sensitivity to cold and my shameless indolence. It was so cosy where I lay and I was so nice and warm by now that I'd begun to like it. And I was to get up and look for a bed for the night somewhere else? My cowardice, turning its back on my conscience, whispered ever so sweetly that I should remain happily where I lay. It convinced me that some kind of unpleasantness was inevitable, and, as long as I was in bed, I could hope that the person would retire to the room opposite and not even notice me. I might be able to make a nice quiet escape in the morning and, unless I gave myself away, they might never know that they had had an overnight guest in their abode.

O, shameless cowardice and unworthy hope! Woe, oh woe! Now I heard a creak on the stairs. I cowered. But then there were two doors upstairs and it depended which one the person selected. However, the rusty door handle squeaked ominously and from that moment my ears could take a rest, for now my eyes alone were employed.

First into the room was a burst of light that fell on the made-up bed, while that on which I lay was still concealed by the shadow of the partly opened door. Then before me shone the flame of a candle. At that I opened my mouth and held my breath.

The flame was as beautiful as the morning star before daybreak and it embraced the wick so tenderly and ur-

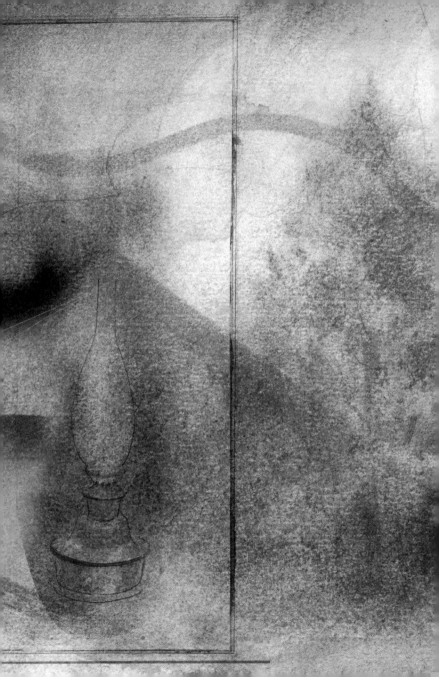

banely that I could have wished to be the one burning. And the candle itself –

Well, it had me bewitched. It wasn't just the wax. It was so unimaginably and inscrutably decorous that I was quite untroubled that a candle so sublime and noble should be ensconced in a primitive holder made of fairly thick, twisted wire with a handle to match. The holder was gripped between the fingers of a hand that seemed to be floating, as in the air or on water, its arm bared to the elbow, and –

Flaming hell! What next!

At that moment, of all the things that might have put in an appearance, surely nothing could more be distressing. A woman, would you believe! What now?

What I would have preferred above all else was to have squeezed myself along under the bed and leapt out of the window. I already had one arm out, then one leg. And? Well, the outlook was bleak. I might have envied the viper and started wallowing in self-pity if the sinister spirit dwelling in my heart had not chimed in:

It'll be that hermit business! Now you've got everything you were looking for. Even a woman. But you're not afraid, are you? Let's be having you, and don't go putting on an act! Won't it be wonderful when she sees a hermit in his nightshirt, weaving all the grace of his spirit into genteel words.

I might almost have grown despondent. My brain failed completely. I'd gladly have taken blows, kicks, being rolled and dragged across the floor and bumped down the stairs and the inevitable fall as an entirely warranted punishment, but I was afraid of shouting and needless words. I'd have crept under the duvet and let myself be strangled. I'd –

As is often the way, my unprincipled fear roused – among all my imaginings – only the most stupid. But in the depths of distress my curiosity also stirred. It had a good laugh and said, as sweetly as possible:

Wait! You know nothing yet. She might be a witch. She might not say anything, just come in and bow to you, sear your nose and nails and fingers with that love candle and leave. Or it's also possible that she won't even glance at you, she might just lock you in like a tomcat in an oven and set fire to the house. Or would you prefer her to lock you in the henhouse with the chickens and give you clucking lessons?

Well, how dismal.

The woman may have meant to close the door behind her. Her shadow slid the length of me much as mine had slid the length of the viper earlier. I felt its cooling touch on both my face and my body beneath the duvet. Certainly she was about to close the door, but I still hadn't had even a glimpse of her non-human features, and, wrestling with my impatience, I could only wonder where an impure witch and the hag of all hags had come by such a pure candle and why, instead of the candle, she hadn't lit either a severed tail or a putrescent limb.

But suddenly, perhaps from habit, she glanced towards where her bed was and from beneath my half-closed lashes I saw a woman fair of form, slim and anything but old, and I saw the sheen of her luminous red hair and a face quite clearly marked by a peculiar mystique that escaped my failing comprehension. And now it struck me that we were separated by the distance of death and the grave and that I needn't be afraid and might look at her even until worn to death. But this was an illusion born of wishful thinking. Now she spotted me, stopped short and took a step back in fright, much as I had when faced with that hideous viper.

I am sure she was repelled by me. And justifiably so. After all, that part of my being that was protruding like a carcass from the duvet was certainly no more appealing than the monstrous disk of that coiled snake. But I dearly wished she would open negotiations and not spend too long thinking about it.

Up to now she'd been standing over me, barely breathing, watching my stupid head as if it were an object that had acquired an unforeseen, if unstable value.

It might have been ludicrous, but above all malevolent. Her eyes now betrayed her first genuine impressions. And how! Well, at that instant she would have preferred above all either to gouge out my eyes or rip out my throat, from which she was deflected by a strange remembrance of some nameless, fathomless terror and some, perhaps genuinely unbearable, heartache, for then it wasn't even a merely human fear and pain, but something more like a mute admission of defeat and reconcilement to rejection.

What next? I would dearly have liked to know whether I was really scary even when asleep. But I'd have had to play hide-and-seek a while longer, and that struck me as slightly inhuman. I was an impediment. And that being so, might not the viper, which had been reposing in its customary spot and had yet permitted me to come this far, be entitled to think itself better than I?

I moved my neck and spoke, believing that it was I myself saying it:

"You took your time!"

I might have seemed to be talking in my sleep, since it sounded more like a cry into the past and the mute darkness. It might also have seemed to be nothing. However, to my amazement my cry didn't go unanswered.

"Do forgive me! I'd no idea a visitor was arriving today."

So the voice was human and entirely intelligible. Its unmistakability was like the whizzing of a stone flying in close proximity to the mouth. But that would only have been a beginning. I was rude enough to raise my forehead like a coiled snake and say with all the indifference that I could muster:

"Where've you been all this time?"

It might have been merely a continuation of what I'd said before, or a sigh, or nothing. But the past replied:

"And were you late and you missed something?"

This now came as a swipe across the face and I would have curled up to conceal my embarrassment, but something kept poking and kicking me, trying to roll me over, until I hissed out loud:

"More than you, that's for sure."

"Oh," she said sarcastically, "you weren't feeling sad, were you?"

What now? I had a vision of a snake being beaten to death. Now I was faced with the same. All right. On we go!

It was dark. Stars of a penitent blue peeped through the window, and the plaintive wind was dressed for a funeral. The waves of the brook continued wailing bitterly over the past, the voices of alders and limes giving

it their timid response. Yes, I had been feeling sad. And more than that –

But there was the candle. It wasn't grieving for anything. It shone more sweetly than the tears of those stars. It knew everything and prompted me itself:

"About the same as you."

That did it. The blood rushed to her face and her jaws twitched. But she had run out of breath and was transfixed, watching me as if I were a hideous apparition. Suddenly she frowned and in a peculiar whine said:

"Do you mean you know?"

"Well," I said, "don't be mad at me! I don't know what drew me here, and why here of all places. I didn't get here till after dark and was so shattered that I just tried to find somewhere to drop down and die. But where were you?"

She blanched, lowered her head, then began to tremble, but suddenly she pulled herself together and snapped:

"Out thieving."

At that point I felt in my limbs that my torpor was passing, as if the sound of that simple word had set the pendulum of a stopped clock swinging. Now it was my jaws' turn to twitch, since my heart had gone wild and I wished I'd been her accomplice.

"And have you brought something?"

I could scarcely have believed that that would win her over. For now she replied much more benignly:

"Didn't you hear?"

"But of course! I get it now. How many?"

"Not a lot. A rooster and two hens. Foxes have probably had the rest."

I would have found this heartening, but something was bugging me. Was this neck of the woods not really as desolate and deserted as it had first seemed? If that were so, it would have been the end of the hermit lark, and caution dictated that I should ask:

"Are there actually people still living here?"

"No. In these parts you won't even see a limping cat. The chickens are feral and they've taken to roosting in trees. I had to wait till darkness fell."

That offered some reassurance, but then I realised that parts of what she was saying were passing her lips only with some difficulty, so I began to test her.

"But you've got a goat as well."

That prying allusion was not to her liking. She replied only reluctantly:

"I'd brought her with me."

"Where from?"

"Over yonder – "

She frowned and gave a toss of her head.

"I see," I said, "and did you bring any other stuff?"

"Yes, on a handcart."

"Really? When?"

"This morning."

"Aha!"

She dropped her gaze and chewed her lip.

"I envy you," I said with a sigh.

"The handcart?"

"No, the sheer delight. It was such a lovely day. The sky above the mountains, the rapturous sun, the forests and shadows! And as you climbed to the skyline, did you not see that around you lay heaven and ahead of you paradise?"

She pulled an odd face and said:

"For you, maybe."

I wanted to change the subject and started in jest:

"Well, honestly, just look! You've got your own house here, you're your own mistress and everything that you need and is already here belongs to you and you alone. And how the numbers grow! You and the goat make two, the cock and two hens – that comes to five. Now you've caught me, that makes me sixth. And all in a single day!"

"Aren't you going to chase me out?"

"What makes you say that? Am I that frightening?"

"But I was born right here, next to you – "

"Really?"

"Can't you tell from my accent?"

"It must be a miracle. It means we've been fated to meet. Yes, that's it. But let's talk about that tomorrow instead. Now I'm too weary."

"Shall I be off then?"

"Why?"

"So as not to be in your way."

"You're not scared, are you? Just look at me! I'm an old man and today so exhausted that I couldn't get up even if the mattress caught fire beneath me! For a strong, spirited girl like you I'd be as easy to fight off as a lame dog!"

Her mouth twisted into an odd grimace suggesting that she did harbour doubts as to my frailty, while not doubting my honourable intentions. Then, so casually that my blood chilled, she said:

"Not that it would matter. It's a long time since I was a virgin."

"Ah!"

Now I knew that I knew her from somewhere, and I stopped seeing her as a shadow that had blown in only to disappear at once, but as something that could not help pursuing me like a blinded smile or thwarted sin. But I wanted to fight back and so spoke, struggling like an ageing magician trying to put a snake to sleep.

"Wait though! Let me tell you something. Today I surprised a viper. It was an old, hideous beast – well, look at me! And I wanted to kill it, but I suddenly felt sorry for something. The snake reminded me of something and so I let it be. So I'm also a viper, old, hideous, world-weary, and if you wanted to, you could kill me. And you wouldn't have to think so long about it as you did a moment back in the doorway – "

She winced, but said nothing, and I went on.

"But, if you'll indulge me, I'll curl up as the viper did under its spruce tree. And even if you were to tread on me, you'd have nothing to fear. I might even lash out or hiss, but I would do you no harm, because even in my deepest sleep I would instantly remember that it was probably you."

I might have calmed myself with these words. I certainly needed to. But she suddenly sat down on the edge of the bed, facing me, and my breath failed me, my heart failed me, and how could my senses have not failed me!

The candle flame lit up all the terrors of my dreams. Her ginger hair, which luminesced at the temples as in the half-light floating around a lamp on a tombstone. Her bluish, shameless, burning eyes, which shone more showily than a sin denied. Her sensuously parted and contorted lips, full of malice and scorn, and on each cheek a peculiar mark, pinkish as a rose petal that had breathed out death. Oh, that ginger hair! What a powerful reminder of wandering forlornly along forbidden and ill-fated paths in those hazy days when I first sensed the approach of temptation! How it struck terror in me! I recoiled from it as an affirmation of my shame and a token of my disinheritance, and I could have endured anything else, believing that even suicide were better and more bearable than the infernal glitter of her brazen hair. For beneath the hair were her no less shameless and profane eyes, and a little way beneath them were her pouting lips and behind those lips the alabaster teeth and behind the teeth lurked a triumphant laughter that gave one the creeps. Without a doubt, those lips would leave a permanent mark on me like caustic soda, those alabaster teeth – aah! Come death instead!

And yet I felt that in that very state of disinheritance lay my entire paradise, all the defiance of my blood and the nobility of rebellion, and in my heart there was a clamouring: Hey, just grab her so that you may, if but for a moment, sink your face in that hair from hell and kiss those lips! Or are you worried about losing your adolescent shyness? Get away! You can just lay bare her lap, then cut her throat and let her bleed out –

No, it was neither shyness, nor divine inspiration that deflected me from temptation, but pathetic fear, and since that day I have preferred to avoid such opportunities. And did avoid them, alas! But now?

Perhaps it was the candle. Perhaps the recollection of that matchless and blissful being that looked down, clinging to the golden gate of God's rainbow, down into my boyhood dreams. But did that matchless and blissful being have ginger hair? And lips like these?

I became despondent and said, offhand, as if I were dreaming:

"But that viper reminded me of something odd."

Her hand twitched.

"What?"

I raised an eyebrow.

"Well, have you ever played the piano?"

She replied, albeit with some reluctance:

"Long ago."

She lowered her gaze.

"Sorry," I said in an attempt to appease her, "I've no idea why I was being so silly as to ask you like that. The viper showed me what hand posture is and what playing is. And what mastery is and glory and composure. But you know all that already."

She sat on the bed, one leg hanging loose, the other resting on the floor. And now the latter slipped. Her body lurched and the candlestick wobbled in her hand.

That disconcerted me and I forgot that I'd meant to stop prattling.

"It wasn't a song that you hear through your ears," I persisted with my prayer for the dead, "it was a miracle! Oh, so beautiful it was! The beast's bearing! It almost brought tears to my eyes. Even though it was so old and hideous. – Won't you lie down?"

Then, in a voice that, despite her best efforts, qua-vered perceptibly, she said:

"But please, won't you tell me who you are?"

"Why do you ask?"

"You're scaring me."

"Why?"

"I'm sure you're kind. But I don't know who you are."

"Now I understand. You think I'm a devil –"

"Oh, no!"

"A devil can also be kind. At least some of the time."

"Stop! Don't be annoyed! I really am scared. You could easily send me packing –"

"Hm! More driving away. I'm beginning to think that that's what you want. But I wouldn't be so oblig-ing. I don't know how to do it and I don't wish to know. But what I would like to know is what you would do if I really did mean to send you packing, now, in the night."

I thought this would discomfit her, but I had seen that she'd been waiting for that very question.

"If you'd let me," she said with an adorable venom, "I'd grab my goat and spend the night with her in the cemetery."

"You can't mean that! The cemetery?

My incautious astonishment gave her some mischie-vous and sardonic pleasure.

"It's quite close," she said casually, mocking the astonishment in my eyes and parted lips.

"Close?"

"Only a few yards. But you came from the opposite direction."

I couldn't fail to be surprised.

"And why there?"

"Towards the end, people didn't dare go there even in the daytime, and I know that even you wouldn't fancy following me there in the dark."

I liked how she put it, but I had to dampen her spirits a bit.

"You'd be wrong there. I'm a gravedigger."

I don't know what she saw in my eyes, but she was genuinely startled.

"I fear, kind sir, that you're making fun of me."

She spoke with a mix of alarmed respect and mortification, but also with such calculated petulance that I understood everything. And I knew not whether to be intimated by it or to laugh at it.

"Well, I can satisfy you on that score in the morning," I replied with at least an appearance of inexorability. "Have you got a pick and spade?"

Now she was reduced to stuttering.

"But what do you want them for?"

And now I realised that I had strayed into the borderlands of Hell. Her fright was bringing back the horrors of recent years, when the living had been forced to dig their own graves. She even suspected me of something of the kind. But I gave nothing away, merely replying with a frivolous and wicked jest.

"Well, what are they usually for? You dig a hole with them and then anything at all can be dumped in it. Obvious, isn't it?"

We were watching each other, sizing each other up. But I felt worse than she. So I said:

"Would you care to accompany me?"

She goggled and suddenly put all her disdain into a grimace.

"That's up to you."

"Really? I'm not so sure. I wouldn't advise it. It's already started to ooze."

She thought I was crazy.

"What are you on about?"

"Hm," I began, ignoring her rising terror, "I was in the next village and I found a coffin in the church, in front of the altar. I don't know what's in the coffin, but it's oozing. They must have forgotten to bury it. They may not have had time to. But aren't you cold?"

She could well have asked the same question of me. The longer I spoke, the more I brought back all the cold horror and odiousness of what was oozing from the coffin.

But suddenly she rallied and said:

"I see now! And you'd like to bury the corpse?"

"Of course. That's why I've come. That doesn't disgust you, I hope."

"And why you?"

"Who else but me? There are no living people around here, and devils aren't going to bring it out for burial."

"And that's the only reason you came?"

"Hm! Does that surprise you? I'm no use for anything else, and a job like this is no worse than what I used to do."

"Yes, I am surprised. I don't know what you used to do, but –"

"Well?"

"You're having me on!"

She said it with such indulgence that my blood boiled.

"So *you* tell *me*: shouldn't *I* be the one to be surprised that *you* want to go to the cemetery at night with that goat!"

She smiled mournfully and said:

"There's nothing else I could do. Rather than head for the border, now, tonight, I'd prefer to be dumped in the hole."

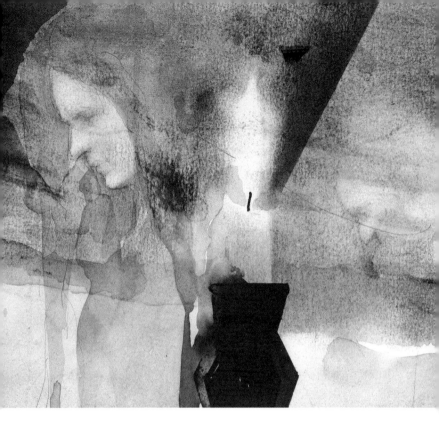

"Why? Are there ghosts that way?"

"Yes."

I stared at her. I guessed that she was around thirty. She could well have been younger, but anger and defiance had incised the first permanent wrinkles into her face.

"Well," I said, "I don't get the impression that you, of all people, scare easily."

"Whether I do or not, it makes little odds. True, it's barely two hours from here to the frontier on foot, it's a bright night and the road is white. But there's a moon tonight."

"Are you a sleepwalker?"

"No, but whenever there's a moon, I can see the dead."

Up to that moment, I'd felt like a catfish lurking in a dark pool into which an incautious minnow had strayed. And now I could see that not even this little minnow was unprepared. I was sure she knew how to muddy the water. I wanted to confuse her and my next question caught her off balance:

"And that's why you'd go to the cemetery?"

"Yes. There are none of those I'd be afraid of there. The ones there are past it."

"So the only people you see are ones who haven't been buried?"

"Not everywhere. Only that way, close to the frontier."

"And why do they haunt you like that? Are they after something?"

"I don't know. I don't want to know and I want to stop thinking about it."

"Are they people you know?"

"My mother and aunt."

"And what happened to them?"

With such pride and truculence that it sent a shiver down my spine, she said:

"They were killed as they fled. And I was there."

The words did not surprise me. The painful thing was that from that moment time turned back on itself. How could it be that accounts of this kind had remained unsettled? Where had she been for so long? In what hell had she been held that she hadn't yet heard that God's rainbow had shone out above the earth?

However, propriety dictated that I should raise the upper half of my body and speak from a sitting position:

"Who killed them?"

Now her face cleared momentarily, but that was only so that it might immediately display such a terrible smile that I regretted not having bitten my tongue.

"Better not ask! I wouldn't want to give offence."

I looked to the side and it struck me that a page in the inviolable Book of Life had been turned back, and I couldn't understand it, because I honestly felt that I was still alive and far from dead. And if that was all! Why was I so upset? Was it my page? Of all that was written on it, nothing related to me, and now I saw that this page was the very one being compared with the page of my own life. Yet I had to sustain a respectful countenance and say as submissively as possible:

"Please, don't mind me! Did anything happen to you?"

And I was trapped.

"Not much," she replied. "They just trod me down and then – I'm sure you can guess."

Her voice was so pure and so beautifully caustic that it was a moment before I wrenched my foot back, believing that I had trodden on the viper that I had already half-forgotten.

She registered it. With contemptuous surprise she fixed her toxically blue eyes on me and even offered me some words of comfort:

"Come! It's not that bad! After all, it wasn't the first or last time. And they were so kind as to make sure I came out of it alive and that they hadn't hurt me. And there were only two of them."

And I was well and truly trapped.

The voice with which she told her tale was one voice on behalf of all. It was quiet and light like suppressed laughter, and I didn't have to understand the words to grasp that if I were ever to escape their terrible spell I would not be the person I had been when I arrived.

"All right," I said, urging her on out of fear of suffocation, she having remained silent as she watched me through her dazzling, piercing eyes, "and how did it happen?"

"Oh, there were so many things like that going on and no one's interested today!"

"Possibly. But this concerns me too."

"Why?"

"Do go on. Please!"

She slightly bared her lip and I thought about whatever was in that coffin. Then she half-closed her eyes and began telling her story.

"In the event, I myself – not to put too fine a point on it – was lucky. Fate allowed me to lie with my eyes facing towards my mother, but only because the one who had his way with me first was pushing his head against me from the other side."

The way she said this was as if she were standing before an examining magistrate, and to reinforce the point she pressed one hand against her temple. Even her voice so adapted itself to her half-closed eyes and the simple, eloquent movements of her hand that I wanted desperately to curl up before her like a coiled snake. But for now I sat with my legs bent uncomfortably and my body erect, and I couldn't move because she was watching me and talking to me.

"And so afterwards," she went on, "I could see the blood streaming from her breast and was surprised that the blood was so dark. That could have been because she was lying in deep shade in a wild, dark forest."

She fell silent and lapsed into a reverie, and I felt faint. But her restless lips remained apart and her body seemed suddenly to be shot through by either a convulsion as at death, or a fantastic, incommunicable and triumphant moment of ecstasy.

"Then I saw," – this came gushing at me like curdled blood right into my face – "the fire in her eyes going out. At which point I completely forgot about what they were doing to me and my only concern was that the man lying on top of me should not move his head to the other side and so hide my mother from me."

It was all toppling and falling on me like a blazing wall and I felt convulsed and faint and terror-stricken and I wished for nothing more than that she first trample me down herself. But then she drew breath and her voice was like a hymn descending from the heights of the Throne.

"My angelic mother just reeled and fell flat on her back before me without even a sigh. And her face was so calm and so unutterably and magnificently beautiful that everything in me went rigid and seethed and screamed with pride and joy. Then I could think of nothing but that not even the worst possible violation could take away that greatest honour of having been and forever remaining her daughter."

Now I had fallen from some great height. So I was unworthy of being trodden down. Except by her! Her alone! And she seemed to be holding me, shaking me and constantly showing me her burning cheeks and menacing lips, though she actually sat there motionless and was speaking with all the serene, sweet trust of a guileless child.

"You may take my word for it that at that moment I wouldn't have dared even to sob! That I gritted my teeth, if only not to spoil the beauty of our farewells. That I was happier obliging the man so that he could lie as comfortably as possible and not have to change position. And I could even have thanked him sincerely for lying in such a way that I could see my mother to the end."

Then she caressed her lovely candle and went off into a reverie. And I felt troubled, but I needed to respond and I said:

"I envy you."

She winced and flared up, whether with anger or shame. Then she blurted out:

"Oh really? Are you a woman?"

"No," I said, "I envy you that parting with your mother."

She drew back her lips, gripped the candle and held her breath. But then, like a minnow fleeing danger, she quickly began muddying the waters again.

"Wait though! I haven't told you everything yet."

"What else?"

"Don't forget I also had to see and hear my auntie. She was hunch-backed, only half-witted and totally infantile. It all terrified her and she didn't want to die, but she was so careless that on the way she seemed to be deliberately doing things only crazy people do. If she'd just walked calmly on without looking back at least, we could have been saved. But what happened had to happen. So when those two caught us by surprise, she started shouting and arguing and not for a second did it dawn on her that they were actually looking forward to shooting a hole in her hump, just for the hell of it. Then as I was being raped, she began howling and screeching in such an unnatural way that it was quite awful. And can you guess what she was on about? The poor creature was afraid they'd go and rape her like they were doing to me. Then the other one, who by then was riding up and down on me, started laughing so violently that I can still feel how it made my intestines and underbelly shake. And I couldn't even move. His paws – what paws they were! And it was happening in the forest and the forest was laughing at me – Even the birds were jeering until the shot rang out, and then –"

I thought she was going to burst into tears. But she had me fooled. She said, as if in jest:

"Do forgive me! I'm like an old woman once I get going, and you want to get to sleep."

That was the last straw. She had fed me with these bitter things as you feed a goose, fit to tear my oesophagus, and now, to wash it all down, she had dashed into my mouth all that cadaverous sludge, whether her own or another's.

"Well," I said, "I'm not sure about that. Probably as much as you do. But do explain one thing to me. After that, do with me as you will. What is it that you don't want to know? What is it that you don't want to think about and are avoiding?"

She could have apparently done without that question. But by this stage she couldn't not reply and she was so proud that she could let no untruth pass her lips.

"My mother."

"Why so?"

"Oh, how little you know," she said with agonising disdain, "you're only a man! All right, she's dead. But why does she persecute me like this? What's she missing? What does she want? Why does she watch me as if to reproach me for not being able to die? Well, it shames and embarrasses me, I don't deny it. But what can I do?"

That voice! Ah, that voice! So resonant it was and so redolent of the pastureland of bees that it hurt inside the eyes and wailed in the bones!

"Are you ashamed," I interrupted her, "of the great miracle of your being alive?"

"Do you mind?" she snapped back. "It's a life I'd honestly be better off without!"

Now I could see, of course, that this was surely a marvel that, because she did not understand it, took on all the more dazzling and astringent beauty. She really was alive. She may have fallen asleep, resting her head against the gates of Hell, and she was not fully awake yet, though she had had to rise and sleepwalk with the carpetbag of her destitution all the way here. But why was she alive? To whom was she of interest and why was it desirable to have her so strangely branded?

But where was I in all this? What conniving spirit had driven me here too? After all, this business wasn't for me, no, it wasn't. I was twitching like a mouse. Me! What was I supposed to be doing here? Yes, she had been quite right to say that I was only a man and she only a woman. And if I wanted to play the hermit, then that was up to me alone.

I swung my legs down from the bed and as I looked for my trousers and boots I said casually:

"That's enough for me. Now I'll draw you up a deed and tomorrow I can bring you certification that this house is yours with whatever else you need for better or worse."

My boots surprised her less than my words.

"Do you have that kind of authority?"

"It's nothing."

"But do tell me, please –"

"What?"

"Why you in particular?"

"I don't know. Perhaps by some dereliction."

"Meaning?"

"That's enough now! I don't understand it either. I meant to act the fool in my old age and do a spot of hermitry. So I came all this way, and that's the dereliction. I can see that now, so I'd better be off."

Then she cried out:

"Where to?"

"I don't know. Anywhere. To Sodsville to spook the demons and crows."

"I haven't offended you. Have I?"

"No. This is your house, your inheritance from your parents, and I have no right to disturb your peace and quiet."

She rose, walked round the bed, came right up to me and held her beautiful candle out to me as if to give evidence under oath.

"Who was it said, in my hearing, that he was so exhausted after his journey that he couldn't get up even if the mattress beneath him caught fire?"

What now?

Ahead of me lay a comfortless and uncertain journey and I needed to tie my boots at least. If only not to have to see that bewitching candle. But something was prodding my chin upwards and something was pulling my eyelids upwards and suddenly I registered her smile, shy, submissive, soliciting my compassion and so painfully beautiful with the kind of compassionate disdain harboured by violated and betrayed women towards all bashful men that it took all the dwindling remnants of my powers to muster the hoarse reply:

"Well, I've had a rest and now I can move on."

Then she cried out:

"You can't go!"

"I have to," I said. "Let me explain. You're seeking peace and quiet, as am I after all. And this way neither of us is going to find it."

"Peace and quiet? Only in the grave, that."

The words didn't so much strike me as kick me. Just what was she, and what I?

But I pressed home my protest:

"I've said my piece."

"Well, we'll see about that!"

And in no time at all I was surrounded by a swirling vertiginous darkness. And I heard the multiple echo of her voice, but in vain I sought my arms and legs. And I would have liked to think about all manner of things, but now I was sprawling back in bed, telling myself that the best I could do would be to put it all out of my mind and sleep on it.

It took me time to grow accustomed to the sapless gloom, in which glimmers of her red hair and toxically blue eyes danced spectrally before my eyes. And now, in the gloom, she took off her dress and hung it up somewhere. Then she sat down with her back to me and donned her nightdress. And as if I had realised where I was and what was happening, my patience began to run out and I would have told her to duck under the duvet and go to sleep, at once. But I could see that this would fail, and I moaned under my breath:

"Some playing the hermit this is going to be!"

She was still sitting on the bed with her back to me. Now she turned and asked:

"Is there anything you'd fancy?"

That stung me. What business of hers was it, what I might fancy! And how could she want me to think about or fancy anything?

"No, nothing," I said, "please, just say your prayers and go to sleep, will you?"

Clearly, I would have liked to fall asleep in order to escape all that was shaking and buffeting me, for all these things far exceeded the narrow confines of what may be encompassed by attentiveness and controlled by willpower. With her mysterious, unappreciated and homicidal dowry, this whole being was now seducing me, drawing me to her so powerfully, brooking no further argument, that she seemed about to have me in her grasp. And why? So that I might see the miracle of her being truly alive? So that I might stand there like an inane witness with only mischief in mind? Or so that I might start praying? For what? For whom? Inside I was a churned-up, blaspheming mess. I cursed my own doltishness and infirmity of purpose. I should definitely have left, even after she doused the candle, for now I could see that this was not for me, no. Oh, no! Certainly not for me!

But sleep was long in coming. I would have liked to think of something more substantial than the errant sparks that were still dying frighteningly in the dead embrace of the darkness. In vain did I seek my unfamiliar self and the overgrown bombsite of my lost youth and the debris that had been my heart. But even now, the only things I could see were those that are indestructible, just passion and heartache. And I would dearly have placed hope in my fatigue, deluding myself that I would finally pass out. But sleep was long in coming.

I stared at the strip of moonlight and suddenly that big, brown viper came back to me.

This time I felt sorry for it. It now seemed more fair-minded and better than I, and I now waited for it with as much trust as if I knew that it would definitely come and I could tell it. This slowly added to my weariness and I might have fallen asleep if I hadn't started, seeming already to sense the viper's presence.

She too woke up and asked, startled:

"What's wrong?"

"Nothing," I said, "I was just dreaming about the viper."

"Me too."

The words frightened me far more than the viper in my half-sleep.

"And?"

"Never mind! Better go back to sleep!"

But how was I to get to sleep? I tried guessing what she might have dreamed about the viper. Though by now I was faint and only my basest senses, ever inclined to mischief, could have responded, and I felt as if I were coiled up between her breasts, and, slowly stretching out my hairless, whitish neck, I brought my head, now resembling an unopened water lily bud disgorged from a suddenly dried-up mud-bed and trodden down for fun, closer to her still unsuspecting and pacific lips. I was still not within range of them and was about to unfurl at least one coil of my ophidian body, believing that I was going do so in such a way that she would feel nothing. But that effort would have also brought my ribs into play, which would, of course, have put added pressure on her chest. I froze, reducing my eyes to slits, and held my breath. She must not wake up! Meanwhile, part of my serpentine body had become so extended that I couldn't hold it there unsupported and it began to sink back. Then I sensed cramp setting in and kept opening my mouth as if I were about to die there and then. Then I was shaken by the urge to weep, but I was only a viper and could have produced no more than a hiss. And then –

In my sleep I must have thrashed out in terror. Then, having woken up, I asked her:

"Are you asleep?"

"No."

"Why?"

"I've just remembered the corpse in that coffin."

I was taken aback. Was she not inducing these monstrous dreams herself? Would she not drive me insane?"

And then I had a flash of inspiration.

"Suppose we go and bury it, right now, tonight?"

"Now? Why?"

"It's cool now and doing it now would be pleasanter and easier than in the daytime. And the corpse might even look quite nice by the light of the moon. And that way we could free ourselves from our oppressive dreams."

"I know. You want to get away."

That was galling. It sank like a needle right into my veins and my nose drooped.

"No," I lied, "I don't."

"That'll get us nowhere. You're worn out. You're also forgetting that you're in the mountains here. By the morning you'd have caught a chill. Then you'd have to stay in bed for goodness knows how long. And now, right now, it's so wonderful!"

This was, of course, a quite serious and incontrovertible argument. That I was sickness-prone was undeniable. If I were here alone –

Well, I mused, if I were here alone, it wouldn't matter. Suppose I did die? What of it? I might even find it amusing. But could I expect her to go to the trouble of caring for me? And where would that lead? Could I have ever got away from the place?

"All right," I said, "I wouldn't want to inconvenience you. Let's see if I can get back to sleep."

And that was that. She said no more, turned on her side and began breathing as silently and calmly as a baby. And the night seemed so beautiful that I might never have lived to see a more beautiful one. There was a glimmering brought about by the pale moonlight, the sweet glitter of tears, the silent trust of the dead and an exalted hankering after unrevealed mercy and future glory. And my heart expanded so powerfully that the blood now sensed a malaise as in the proximity of death, and I wished I might metamorphose into the frame of that steadfast window, through which, on happy days, the girl's eyes would twinkle joyously from within and at night the stars would peep in from without, or into one of the beams that held the ceiling up, full of wisdom, omniscience and a soulful beauty. And the stars watched me, twinkling eyes, and the beams woke up, but they said nothing –

Within touching distance, there she slept, next to me, she whose body and soul had been scarred by all the horrors of violation and acute shame, which had surely twisted all her vital organs, uprooted all the buttresses of her heart and shredded her gullet. What was she, this being? She had come in secret, scared even of her own shadow, and yet she *had* come, doubtless bringing with her more pride and self-confidence than clothes and underwear, perhaps even knowing that, were she to stay, she would drop down and die here like a mangy mouse. And she wanted to stay and she would have sacrificed her tortured body and wounded modesty if only to redeem the air of the place of her birth, a stretch of skyline bounded by two arms of the mountains, and the bed of her mother. How she had undressed by the light of the moon! And why, oh why, had she not wanted to let me go!

So what was I supposed to want? It is not impossible to flee from temptation. But flee from her? That would have given the devil something to laugh about! And then – had she not shamed me with those fundamental virtues of which I was in such short supply? What was she, and what was I, eh? I'd been brought here by the urge to rebel, cloaked only shabbily in senile contrition so as to put a smug gloss on its pitiful shadow. And why had she come? Oh, why think about it? I could have wept at my wretched self, for now I saw that next to her I had so little to commend me.

But at that very instant there flashed before my eyes a clear revelation of being at the very spot on which my gaze had focused ever since the day when the glory of the firmament and the stars had first bounced off my awestruck eyes and towards which my impotent longing had been turned, flapping its wings in vain like a legless bird. A revelation of having reached my destination, which was more dangerous than I would ever have guessed. And only now was I overtaken by fear. For it reached up to the dizziest heights of light. And it looked down into the most terrible depths of darkness. What was it? And how had I come thus far?

My reason afforded me no answer. Some spirit may have meant just to have a little fun and had seized me, leading me as a sleepwalker up to the top of a church's dome. And now I had woken up. Oh, how magnificent and exalted it was! I was awash with the cool glow of the moon and it was dizzying, dizzying. The wonder! The awakening! The glory! That unbearable and petrifying beauty! Onward! Ever onward! Even if only to come crashing back down!

What was I to do, whom to ask? The place where I found myself brooks no parley. Whoever reaches this far can never go back. And now I seemed to be falling –

And the hand of her who was resting there beside me twitched as if seeking to hold back from some peril. Whether asleep or awake, she was looking for something, reaching out to my face. And the hand seemed to be afraid, so I took it, kissed it and tucked it in again.

She may truly have been asleep, since thereafter she didn't stir, while I couldn't get to sleep for a very long time. But if there was fear in me, it was not of her, but for her. Only for her. After all, now I would have, even in the extreme of lassitude, to harbour a constant sense that, one way or another, I should stumble on in her footsteps towards my appalling destination.

The morning was so murky that the frames round the window panes etched themselves on my timorously waking consciousness like the bars of a prison cell. The window probably didn't fit properly any more. Mist was seeping in and slowly exhaling a peculiar, miserable cold like an autumn rose coated in hoarfrost. Then I also saw, stirring in the haze, someone's hands and hair and a face, and that was proof that this was not a dream, that I really was trapped with no means of escape.

I must have woken the same time as she. She was getting changed as I rose, calm and carefree, turning only slowly to face me. I bowed, wished her good morning and then just froze.

She clasped her shift to her at the waist, but there was now no room in her eyes for any hint of coyness or unease, or for that dismissive, acerbic disdain. She could have stood like that in judgement before God. What was done was done. There was no more need of tears, or defiance, or fear or shame, let alone the shift.

It wasn't fitting, however, that I should stand there, gawping at her like a bleary-eyed eagle owl, and I would have started dressing if she hadn't spoken:

"So what did you dream about?"

It needn't have been more than a friendly greeting. But what should I have replied? I was loath to tell the truth and I didn't dare lie.

"You know. Just silly things."

"What kind? Nice or nasty?"

"I don't know."

"Am I permitted to know what you call silly?"

I needed to discover whether she could tell that I had kissed her restless hand in the night and whether she meant to test me.

"I won't say," I replied, "but I'll show you if you want."

I calmly crossed to her, took her by the hand, turned her round and kissed her.

She flushed. I too. And how! Suddenly abashed, I dashed from the room and, disregarding everything, I ran out of the house right down to the water's edge.

There was still a mist, quite dense, the ground was ice-cold, the water black. When, shaking with annoyance and exhausted from running, I suddenly tripped and slipped in such a ludicrous fashion that the crayfish must have had a good laugh, I knew that I was doing something really mindless. But the very idea of going back hit me with such a force of shame that I cast off my shirt with hasty resolve, failing to notice how far I had sent it flying, and then I was lying on the bottom.

I'm not entirely certain how I hauled myself out. My raw and horror-stricken senses couldn't cope even remotely. I know that not even my teeth were up to chattering the way they desperately needed to, that my legs had gone so stiff that they were tripping over each other, that I fell over, got up and then plumped down again, that I was even crawling on my knees and looking and groping and incapable of telling which way round my shirt was, let alone which arm went in which sleeve, since the moment I tried to solve this apparently simple, but actually tricky move, the cold didn't so much set me shivering as it swung me about with such violence that I looked rather less like a hermit and more like a goat with its legs tangled in its tether.

Then I heard a disagreeable and menacing shout, which I must surely have heard before if the noise of the water hadn't drowned it out. I could see nothing. I had just been pulling my nightshirt over my face, but it had clung to my shaking wet nose, and despite all my admonishing refused to uncling itself. Then I flew into a rage and stamped my feet and hopped up and down. By which stage she had joined me.

Her voice was shaking with exasperation and I would have been ashamed of myself if there'd been time. Meanwhile she, standing beside me and unceasing in her castigations, started rubbing me down and stripping me like a rabbit for the skinning, drying me off with something coarsely abrasive, and I have no idea how she then helped me into my shirt and drove me back indoors. How gladly would I have manifested my embarrassment, whether by word or deed, but she drove me so hard that I tripped over the threshold, and then she kept prodding me onwards like some stupid animal until I was back to where, moments before, I had risen to my feet. Then she swathed me in my duvet like an infant, adding her own duvet for good measure, and strictly enjoined me – under pain of disfavour – not even to think of poking my nose out until she herself said that I might.

I tried to stutter at least a couple of words of apology, but she'd disappeared. All I heard was a creak on the stairs and I wanted to be ashamed, there being nothing more agreeable than complacent shame counterbalanced by contentment. But my feet were cold, which was inconvenient, since I wanted to be ashamed with my whole body. So I began to rub one foot against the other in the belief that warming the body would ultimately warm the frozen shame, but this was so wearing that I fell asleep.

When I opened my eyes, it was day, a golden day. And I would have rejoiced, had something not disquieted me, and I would dearly have liked to know whether I hadn't slept through the whole day, the whole night and possibly even my own death. How else could I have explained coming to in such a flood of light and warmth and fragrance! Before, as I was falling asleep, it seemed that the whole day would be murky and dismal. And now?

She was standing beside me. She was girt winsomely with a white apron, rubicund as rapture ensnared and looking at me with such sincere wickedness, as if she could still see me as I had stood before her quite naked and shaking and wet and stiff, then tottering as I struggled with my nightshirt when it got caught on my smug nose. Her red hair had been combed and coiffured and was laughing like that time when she'd looked out –

Ah, was it she? But who was I? She was aglow with contentment and youth and happiness. But what was this that she'd brought me? On a pewter tray decked in snow-white lace was a gilded mug full of steaming goat's milk and a gilded plate laden with still warm fritters. And I looked at her and I knew not where I was, what was happening and how it had come about that all I could see were roses, dew and Maytime. And instead of shame I felt only a sinful and sacrilegious satisfaction, since I could never have hoped to play the hermit so agreeably in my old age.

But I wanted to know if I had overslept. I asked her:

"What's the time?"

She looked round and said:

"You've got a watch. Have a look!"

Her smile confused me and I reached for it apprehensively.

It had stopped.

It might have meant nothing, but I went numb. What if more than just my watch had stopped! Had its stopping not been joined perhaps by time stopping, and was I now as in a maze with no way out?

She briefly watched my discomfiture with merriment, resting her arms on her hips. Then she said:

"Where are you in such a rush to get to?"

"To fetch that certificate to say you can stay here."

She looked grave, turned away and looked towards the sun.

"It's about half past ten."

"That's unfortunate."

"What?"

"That I won't be back till after dark."

"So let's go tomorrow. You'll let me come too, won't you?"

"And what day is it?"

"You don't even know when you got here?"

"Yes, I do. Monday."

She burst out laughing.

"I see you think it's Wednesday. But I wouldn't let you. You can get up now."

And she trotted out, smiling, and the door clicked to and the stairs creaked. All this attested to the fact that I had not been dreaming.

Having had a bite to eat, I dressed and unpacked my rucksack. I took downstairs whatever belonged in the kitchen and begged permission to have a little look round the house.

It seemed very nice. This could have been because the sky had brightened and I didn't have to worry about anything. In particular the beamed ceilings and attic spaces invited one irresistibly to dream, the sunlight coming through the quite small-paned windows doing little more than screen them in a delicate glow. And there was a smell of wood and hay and times past – with their coy remembrance of the scent of balsam, fading lilies and long-stored bedding. Next I explored the lofts and looked nosily into some chests that contained old weaving spools, then I set up a ladder and clambered up into the dormer window. And I saw birches and alders and ashes exposing their first yellowing leaves, steep, tree-clad hillsides, cottage roofs and the sky and clouds –

Oh, how strange it was now in the daytime! Again the sun was shining bright, a golden sun, and it radiated warmth and smiled down as if time had suddenly turned back, as if summer had suddenly come back with its storms and flowers. It was all just so sad, so very sad! But unspeakably beautiful.

Then to the side, through the branches of the birches, something glinted and I saw a cross set on the spike atop a slender spire. Surely the spire of a mortuary chapel. Then it felt as if I had escaped without permission from my coffin or grave and that now I was standing in the dormer like a ghost, looking out and not knowing how to get back or whether I wasn't going to be chased off by a rook or the gravedigger's dog.

But now she was calling. She had made our lunch and so had a moment in which to show me round.

We set off. With rising melancholy I took stock of the empty, fairly large stables with their stone troughs, outhouses containing rusting implements, a woodshed full of uncut timber, a threshing floor and a henhouse. I wanted to pat the goat, but it was so full of distrust that it jumped to one side without even bleating at me.

Then she led me into the garden. I looked at the weed-infested flowerbeds, the crayfish-straggly trees, neglected shrubs and flowers past their best. And suddenly I spotted a rosebush.

It bore only two blooms. One closed, stiff and waking laboriously through a quivering of dew and the sunlight that was insidiously discomposing its tumescent lips, the other wide open and unfurled too far already. And as if something had just given me a nudge, I stepped up close and would you believe it, the petals of this second bloom stirred as if something unseen was breaking them out of their receptacle; I held out my hand but was barely able to catch all that abandoned beauty being shed so painfully. Two petals did fall to the ground and I had to pick them up. Then I was holding them in the palm of my hand and she was watching me, watching and trying to say something, but nothing issued from her lips, and then she may have thought of something else to say, but that didn't come out either, until finally she exhaled as after a severe spasm:

"Who are you?"

I grimaced and said:

"I wish I knew."

"Can I try to guess?"

My heart jumped. But that at least told me that she hadn't been through my papers, and I said boldly:

"Could be fun."

But then she looked at me in such a way that I didn't know which way to jump, and then it came:

"Are you a priest perhaps?"

I felt as if my head had dropped off and that I'd had
to bend down and pick it up shamefaced, but then was
too afraid to put it back on in case I put it on crooked,
and I didn't know what to do with it or whether it was
even my head, or whether I'd ever had a head at all.
And it felt strange to be still able to look at her when I
had nothing left above my shoulders, and as I choked

with embarrassment I had to make at least a pretence of fighting back.

"Goodness, what on earth gave you that idea?"

"Don't dodge the question! Are you? Aren't you?"

I held out my hand so that she might see the smooth gold ring.

"I'm a widower."

"What of it? Once a priest, always a priest."

"Do you honestly think," I protested, "that I would commit sacrilege for the sake of this ring?"

"No, I wouldn't think that. But if you're not a priest, you surely should have been one."

"Maybe," I said, "it pains me and I regret it."

"So why aren't you?"

In my humiliation I crumpled the rose petals still held in my hand.

"I might have become one. But then I thought I needed a kind of trial run, so as not to be acting out of ignorance, until I could see what was on the other side. What use would it have been to me if I'd turned up back then like some unweaned and dehorned bull who on his first appearance would have taken fright at a nanny goat? So I wanted to set off in search of experience and visit the devil. And so I did."

"How did you get there?"

"That's the least of it!"

"What did he say?"

"Oh, he didn't have time. He had me look into a mirror and when I saw my nose in it, that was enough."

"Humph!"

"Should I have gone back?"

She raised her head.

"Why not?"

The rose petals dropped from my hand.

As if she had seen in that the answer to her question, she stared at the fallen petals and I felt faint.

"And why did you come here?"

Her voice sounded so beautiful that the rusting bolts of my heart quaked, grated and began to wail.

"Come on, now, look at me! I'm so old that even common sense advises me to devote the worthless time between now and my death to searching either for virtues or other such unpleasantnesses. And my heart? It tells me: Where else but here! It really is so lovely here!"

"I don't know what it is you're making fun of –"

"My destitution."

"But why?"

"The sins I committed have been borne away by the devil. I don't have to repent of those. But what about those not committed yet?"

"Well, would you like t–? Do you hanker after them?"

"Ah! Ever since I made out the first stars in the sky."

"And now?"

"The only reason I came was to be able to consider, in peace and solitude, here among the mountains, whether I really am so old as never to be perked up by the seven unclean spirits or whether I might still enjoy playing the odd trick and raising hell."

"And what would you like?"

"Oh, all sorts of things! There'd be an awful lot, and I know that the devil's already having a good laugh. But let him! I'm glad to have him."

"But what do you need him for?"

"What would I be without him, and who would harry me?"

"So why do you call him such a nasty name?"

"Huh! He likes it."

She looked at me and smiled indulgently. I squirmed. But I wanted to get it all out.

"Just as long as – now, look! I *am* old enough to be sensible. However, I've never yet managed to find in the world something that would make me feel dizzy, something that might either give me a sting or cast a spell over me –"

Her eyes looked up and with an implacable expression of strangled defiance stared up to the mountain ridge. And my eyes misted over and I was smothered by my own shame, but I still hadn't said the main thing, the most difficult thing –

"Until here and now!"

She tossed her head, then looked with a grimace at the crumpled petals, but said not a word.

I might have bent down and gathered them up. But I thought that first I should gather my lost head, and I felt as I had that time by the stream, stark naked and unable even to look her in the face. But I was still standing there, whether with my head or without it, and at least I stuttered:

"Just as long as I'm here! It really is so beautiful! As if we'd come out of our tomb and seen on each other's face all the things we'd done in the place where we'd had to live, including things that used to make us sad, but are now over. And we're here all alone, just us, you and I, as if we're to be interrogated together and tried, with you taking responsibility and pleading for me, and I in turn for you. Do you know now what I want?"

Nothing. She turned away without a word and I could dream.

I contemplated the apple trees, weighed down with little red-streaked, barrel-shaped fruit. On the ground around them there were so many windfalls that the grass was like a red carpet. There was no one here to gather them up. Close by the apple trees the windows of a low, half-demolished cottage were basking in the sunlight with no one to look out of them. As I was pondering whether, instead of wilted rose petals, I oughtn't to have been gathering the apples up into a pile, it suddenly struck me that I was being watched first by the windows of the half-demolished cottage, then by the apple trees, and the expressions of the windows and the trees were growing ever more bewildered. I stared at the apples lying in the grass and saw that now they too were watching me, watching, and smiling in an odd way. Then some children, resembling the little apples, seemed to be looking out of the cottage windows and wanting to come out to play, but they were so happy that they couldn't catch their breath. And high up beneath the clouds a smile was swaying and the sky was also watching the scene, watching, and a little bird was flitting about happily and twittering contentedly. I picked one apple up, stroked it and put it to my mouth. It alone refused to look at me even out of the corner of its eye and I had to plead:

"Why won't you smile?"

Nothing. Silence. Even the bird suddenly fell silent and vanished, and all the apple trees metamorphosed before my eyes into cloudy spectres of death. Their leaves and fruit suddenly took on a ghostly, unreal aspect and if I had shaken any one of them, it would surely have just rustled mournfully and the ground beneath it would have been covered in brown-withered leaves and rotten fruit. And the children in the windows likewise changed into pale phantoms of corpses and became faceless, as if someone with nothing better to do had raised them up into the embrace of death, then, weary of the game, had let these half-resurrected and startled children be snuffed out again. And now I also lost faith in the fresh and fragrant air, and even more so in the oh-so-benignly smiling sky, to which it would have been pointless to lift my gaze, given that it was in thrall to damnation and death.

So that was the smile that I had been waiting for!

I so wanted to look round for her, but was put off doing any such thing by the fear that she too might change on the instant into the same kind of wraith. So I stood there and dreamed on.

Would I have let her go perhaps? No. I would not. I would stay here with her and I'd go haunting with her. And be very happy to! Whether from derangement or –

From what–?

Ah –

I dashed the apple down on the ground. Not like this! Where would that get me? I would frighten only her.

But now she called over:

"Didn't it taste nice?"

She was standing up a slope, watching me and not believing her eyes. And I would certainly have been embarrassed if she hadn't stepped right up to the nearest apple tree, picked an apple and sunk her teeth into it to check for herself whether it was nice or nasty. Heedless of either shame or sense, I went over to her, snatched the apple from her and began to eat it.

It wailed at me and spoke inside my mouth and it smelled like mementos of the deceased that have been kept in an old trunk. And it was so sweet, oh so humbly sweet like a kiss following seduction! Once it had gone, leaving only the aftertaste of her moist lips in my mouth and the warming prints of her clamped fingers, my eyes opened and I suddenly appreciated how old I was by comparison.

But it was so wonderful! Oh, so wonderful!

Towards the north, the slope merged into a steep embankment that constituted a fairly high, rocky and insurmountable boundary line, half-overgrown with bracken and young birch trees. It led towards a downward sloping panhandle of forest and concealed everything beyond it like the boundary of dreams. There might have been nothing beyond it but a bottomless chasm and the inverse of the sky that was emitting above us nought but felicity and repose. That border-line! Oh, that borderline!

I gazed up towards the forest and spotted that the line led towards a hollow way that looked more like a gully than a track, and suddenly it dawned.

"Is this the way you were going?"

She may have been expecting the question. Quite calmly she replied:

"Yes."

"Good. Come on then."

"What do you want there?"

"Think! I want to find and bury her, I'll have a cross erected on the spot, and after that we'll see."

"It's too soon."

"Why?"

"You'll have second thoughts."

"Hm!"

"Do you know me? Do you think you know what I am?

"Whether I do or not, what difference does it make?"

"Wouldn't you like to?"

"As you will."

"Come on then."

I followed her and we climbed up to the high boundary line, then headed not for the forest, but to the village, skirting overgrown fields and peeping inside abandoned cottages. Those who'd abandoned them clearly hadn't had time to take even the barest essentials with them, and the sundry crops that had been waiting for their husbandman to take them away had become overgrown. This all stimulated my attention, calculation and genuine interest and I might have begun discussing what to do about it, but at that very instant I spotted a quite different kind of two-storey, brick building of regular, sober lines, which definitely fascinated me with its air of officialdom. But what came breaking through its windows was a peculiar, suffocating darkness, and painfully reflected off them were the golden rays of the sun like the glitter of tears that couldn't go dry. Seized by some premonition, I paused and would have gladly frozen and gone off into a dream.

"Is that the school?"

"Yes," she sneered, screwing up her face.

"Why the scowl? Is it where you went to school?"

"Yes, it is."

"Can we go inside?"

"What for?"

"Can't you guess? I want to see and hear you there and imagine you as a schoolgirl."

She frowned.

"Why?"

"Don't you know?"

"I do. But – All right. If I must. As a schoolgirl. That's what they used to call me – Schoolgirl. You see the point – my hair! But I was top of the class! Yes, I left with honours."

"Do you mean they gave honours at this school as well?"

"Humph! At this school! It's not that simple – This school stands in for all schools. I mean stood. Anyway, I had a good time here and didn't even have to pay. They even paid me."

"Oh, I'm sorry. I wasn't prepared –"

"I wasn't prepared either. It hit us so suddenly, everything that happened being done to order with no romance. They just sent in witnesses and a warrant and so it started."

"How did they arrive?"

"In properly official style. It was towards evening and mother and I were indoors and not looking out because by then *they* were already everywhere. You know, *their lot*. And they had their warrant with them. Though not actually *them*. That special honour fell to *our lot*. And they read from it to me: that there was some kind of ordinance from earlier times, and that I had to do this and that, and if I refused, they'd use force. My mother offered to go in my stead, but the one reading the warrant wouldn't hear of it and said that the names

had been drawn fairly by lot and that she should look whose name headed the list. So I went. Just to calm my jitteriness I asked the two men what work I would be given, but neither replied. I found that strange, but I wasn't yet disheartened and told myself that our folk are our folk and they wouldn't let me down. Then in the distance I saw some more girls, also accompanied by our people. But by then we'd reached that cross. And at that point I got so scared that I quickly crossed myself, surreptitiously so no one could see. I've never crossed myself since."

"And what had scared you like that?"

"Everything. Their people, the school, then our people, but mostly perhaps the beautiful sky. It was so bright, just as you see it now. Shining so graciously, slyly, sweetly and tenderly that my jaws quivered and I was swallowing saliva. Though back then it was Maytime and the branches of the trees bent only to the weight of their blossom. And then it started. The shouting, the pounding feet, the bringing out and stacking up of desks, then cleaning the walls, general tidying, fetching straw, in short all the preparations for accommodating our very good friends, in the process of which it was only our people who were chivvying us along and it seemed to me they were doing more than they needed to in setting us an example of diligence and conscientiousness. Well, our folk are ours! Credit where credit's due! Then they left without saying good bye and even locked us in so none of us could run away. And if you happen to want to know what I was feeling, I should have to say nothing. Except perhaps the heat and nausea."

"But memory! The memory! That's the thing, isn't it?"

"Yes, it's that devil. Mine, and the most affectionate one. The one I sleep with."

"Well, be grateful to him!"

"But we do understand each other! And that was the thing about it, how it came out of the blue. Before

I realised they were coming, they'd burst in and taken the precaution of closing the windows, even though it was so sickening that my ears were buzzing. Then there was much clattering and banging and clanging as a signal to those who were to do the deed, and they hadn't even explained what they wanted from me, and then came the nuptials and wedding night."

"So quick and dispassionately?"

"Oh, no. There was such confusion that I can't give you an ordered account of how things went. With each of us it was different, seven of us from the village had been drawn and it was a bit like a cattle market. So when they came at us, one started kicking and smashing things, another started whimpering, trying to cover her eyes and crotch, then a fight broke out and straw was flying everywhere and clouds of dust, then there was a sudden clatter, then a window got smashed, and we all started screaming as if by command."

"Why?"

"One girl had managed to leap at the window and smash both panes with her head. But she caught her throat on the broken pieces and couldn't get out or back and she bled to death. They may have meant to leave her there in full view like a trapped mouse, but then there was such a racket outside as well that they did extricate her and removed her from the room instead."

"And you?"

"Why do you ask? You can see me, can't you? I didn't die and that's why I'm here."

"But you wanted to, didn't you?"

"Well, it didn't happen, so why discuss it? I know I felt as if I my throat was full of glass and straw and dust, that I was falling, then on the ground with someone tramping all over me and strangling and flaying me. Then death passed me by, and when I came to, I was no longer a virgin."

"And what was your consort like?"

"Goodness! There were so many of them. One would be still holding me, not yet finished having his way with me, and the next one would be standing there urging him to get on with it. And you can't imagine all the other fun we had, the screaming and the beatings! No, our village hadn't seen a wedding like that for over three centuries. This one ran non-stop for a week."

"Enough!"

"But afterwards! Waking up from it all! Not a thing in sight. It was all over. The dust and ruined clothes was all they left behind. What now? Let's not go rushing into things! Now? What did now mean? This was forever. Where to go and hide? Though why? You're already holed up with nowhere to go. How about just dying? Ah! Would that help even? The shame? What does shame mean? Nothing. Choke it back. If you spit it out, the harder it will be to pick it up and put it back in your mouth. Come on, it's not that bad and you can count your blessings that you're in hell. Only hell! So, as I was sinking to the very depths of my shame like a worm in a bog, our lot showed up, and do you know what they brought with them? – Our wages for the week!"

"Oh, brilliant! And did they want a receipt?"

"Of course. Rules is rules and to hell with prudery! But I wasn't going to give them the satisfaction."

"What did they say?"

"Oh, they tried to talk me round. Said I should take the money. If I didn't give them a receipt, people might accuse them of embezzlement. And what did I want, they asked. I'd had a good time, they said, hadn't paid for a thing, and did I have any idea how many good, honest women were heartily envious of me? But aren't you hungry?"

"No."

"I can tell you are. Come and have some lunch."

We went. Our shadows followed us, trudging in the shining dust and bumping into each other like exhausted horses. I looked back several times, unable to gaze my fill of the school, and each time the shadows bumped into each other. So we reached the spot where an iron cross rose from its stone plinth.

"Could this be the cross where you crossed your-self?"

"Yes."

Something reached out and touched me and I was impelled to go and kiss the stone in which it was set. And then, heedless of her surprise, I took her unasham-edly by the hand.

"Tell me about how you came back home this way."

First she flinched, then had to swallow her saliva and if I hadn't kept a firm grip on her, she would have snatched her hand from mine.

"I was in no state to take anything in. I was with our people. That's to say they accompanied me. But nothing has left any impression on me. They walked and talked. All I did was look at the fence posts and I didn't even think about meeting my mother."

"Perhaps that was for the best."

"You're right. I think I'd have preferred to hide from her in the barn. But they escorted me as a corpse to the grave and at least ensured that I entered the parlour and listlessly set about my customary work. Mother said nothing. Even then she saw me as an innocent victim cast on the mercy of brutes and tried to defend me. But I was too ashamed to look her in the eye, until she was actually dying. But by then she couldn't see me. She died too quickly."

"You mean she didn't see you and those two –?"

"No. I'm sure she didn't."

"But you've told me about the solemn beauty –"

"Oh dear! By then death was staring from her eyes."

"And did you want her to see?"

She tore herself free.

"You're worse than –"

She sobbed and her mouth contorted.

"Why are you crying? Do tell me and you'll feel better."

"Yes. If she *had* seen it back then, I wouldn't have to be so scared of her. But you know that anyway! You can read it in my face."

"But I wanted to hear it."

"Why?"

"It's so wonderful that I want to eat and drink and breathe my fill of you, even if it makes me choke."

"Oh do you! Steady on though! Later I serviced your lot."

"Well, go on."

"Have it your way then! After they killed her, they left her where she fell, but they took me with them and were so kind as to help me carry her bundle and suitcase and on the way they explained how sad I was going to feel now, alone at home, so they'd try to find a different, more appropriate place for me, where I would have so much fun that I wouldn't even think of escaping. And so it was."

"And?"

"There I serviced three gentlemen of quality. At first I was afraid of them, but then it became a habit."

"How can you say that?"

"Don't you believe me?"

"No. You'll never convince me."

"You only want to hear things that arouse compassion? No! I wouldn't dream of misleading you. I can't go keeping back things that arouse disgust."

"There we go! You've just shown you're confusing terms. Do you know what habit is? It's no laughing matter. It stays in the blood and nothing can undo it."

"Just wait! There's all sorts more still to come –"

"So much the better."

"Meaning?"

"Come on, now! Are you really capable of such cheap lies, walking upside-down, twisting your head and spine and defecating in your own face? It's not that easy. Only the afflicted can do that and you're not one of those."

"How can you know that?"

"It's not just in them. It runs in families. For that you'd have to come and take lessons from us."

"Wait a minute, forgive me, aren't you afraid to say such things so callously, so bluntly?"

"Oh, I'm sorry if it shocks you. Did I say I hold it against them?"

"But they're your people! And it's all the more disturbing that you're saying this to me!"

If in exchange for these words I'd clasped her at once to my heart, she couldn't have resisted. But I didn't dare. I cried:

"Just as disturbing as your claim that it became a habit! That much would be obvious at first sight, even if you were dead. But I've been looking at you now for so long and all I can see is how chaste and beautiful you are."

"Oh please! You must think I'm mad!"

"Hm, mad! I think you'd like me to be!"

"But can't you figure out what it might be like to be in service to three masters?"

"All right, give me a hint. Did they all live in the same house?"

"How could it be otherwise!"

"And did they get on?"

"Like ferrets in a sack."

"And did they beat you?"

"Sometimes."

"Why?"

"From rage, for fun, but mostly from jealousy."

"Brothers?"

"Brothers and their father."

"Were they married?"

"Divorced. Or wanted to be. I never found out."

"Aha! And you?"

"I was having fun. I titillated them and tried to do them as much harm as possible in the process."

"Quite right too. That was presumably your only means of self-defence."

"But not against what you're thinking of. That might be forgivable. The worse one feels, the less one wishes to die. But this wasn't that. No. It wasn't. I was defending myself against my mother."

"Were you actually afraid of her?"

"Yes. Later, only her. Her eyes pursued me wherever I went, constantly reproaching me: What on earth are you doing? But she never offered me any guidance, least of all when I was feeling so bad that I could almost have cursed her. And whenever she seemed to be asking what I was doing, my blood boiled and my entire inner being began to scream: Come and watch if you want, and you can do it instead of me! And at moments like that it wasn't fear of the men that made me compliant, but loathing for her."

"You only think that."

"Do you mind –"

"Oh but I do! It wasn't her, I'm sure. No. It wasn't. You mustn't go thinking that she would be so unjust and wicked and evil. The fear only came from your loving her so much –"

She glanced at me, her eyes blazing. But we'd just reached the footbridge and I had to let go of her and cross, at her bidding, ahead of her. I stared into the water, recalling how I'd felt as I stood before her naked, unable even to look her in the face, then how she'd driven me indoors and I'd fallen asleep, and finally how I came round in the full glare of the sun. And on we went, on and on, and although she was behind me, I could see her, floating ahead of me, her face turned towards mine, girt winsomely with a white apron, rubicund as rapture ensnared. Her red hair was combed and coiffured and was laughing like that time when she –

I gave a shudder. Not like this. It wouldn't do. Not one bit.

I half-closed my eyes and saw her walking like a shadow, looking at the fence posts, or more likely at their shadows, not even thinking of the meeting with her mother, from whom she would probably have hidden in the barn. Only by escorting her as a corpse had they at least ensured that she entered the parlour –

This had to end before we entered the parlour. I pulled her up with a question:

"Is that all now?"

Her thoughts must have wandered off somewhere and came back to me only slowly. Grudgingly she replied:

"Wasn't that enough?"

"There's nothing more to follow?"

That did it. My jaws snapped shut.

"Only a baby."

That voice!

The tremor in it reminded me of the laughter of a pebble jammed right in the middle of one's lips. It was lucky that I grabbed hold of the door handle! But my innate inquisitiveness led me to raise my forehead like a coiled snake and knock her back with a question:

"A boy?"

Her hearing may have sharpened, but she kept the game going, and as if she had again lobbed a sharp-edged stone at me, a cackling laugh now got me in the teeth:

"Only a girl."

Slowly I turned, slowly, staring first at her feet, then higher and higher. And I stood there and stood and after a breathless pause began slowly, so slowly:

"And where do you keep her?"

She opened her eyes wide and as we watched each other it might have seemed to be not us, but two ghosts, each coming from a different hell. And I leaned against the door handle as if not meaning to let her escape inside, and I pursued my interrogation:

"Why didn't you bring her with you?"

She caught her breath, gave a dismissive wave of the hand and heaved a sigh:

"Oh, the child has no knowledge now."

"Is she already dead?"

Her reply was to lower her gaze.

"And where's she buried?"

"In the place I came from."

I wanted to say something. But what? Surely this had to end somehow. But how? I paused for thought and suddenly it all became jumbled inside my head and I couldn't focus my mind on anything, anything. What now? How had she put it? Yes, I was sure she hadn't been speaking for herself alone. She had said it to save me the trouble. Now? Hardly just now! This was forever. Where could I go and hide away? Though why? You're already holed up with nowhere to go. Come on, it's not that bad and you can count your blessings that you're in hell. Only hell!

Aha, that's how it is! Hell! And alone in it with her forever. And watching her and quivering and quaking. But could I have had anything more wonderful in some other place?

"I suppose it had to be," I said, sighing aloud. "But do you realise that I shall miss the little girl now?"

"You? Why?"

"She was yours."

I opened the door for her, but we exchanged not a word more until lunchtime. I had to avoid her and compose myself by recalling my half-forgotten childhood years. That did little to help. Still peeping out from somewhere was that girl, looking into my boyhood dreams from the golden gate of heaven's rainbow and playing at hide-and-seek. And my eyes watered like an old dog's – but then she called me:

"Come and eat."

What should I have done? The clouds that, a moment before, had billowed out like ghosts had now withdrawn, leaving on her face no more than a faded grimace, and I sat at lunch like an inadvertent guest, dumbstruck by the realisation of my geriatric infantilism, for only now did my eyes open wide and I felt apprehensive. No matter how modest a lunch it was, for one who had come here truly seeking the hermit's way it was an unseemly luxury. The table bore a cloth. The crockery, of which I am sure the finest pieces had been chosen, glistened and gleamed. There was even a jar with some flowers in it. And then there was that being with the red hair, clear blue eyes and a little petal of rose or sweet brier on each cheek, and she floated hither and yon, turning towards me and rubicund as rapture ensnared. And that day was very hot, but where I was sitting was pleasantly shaded and the cuckoo in the old wall clock above my head cuckooed:

You're glad you're in hell, right?

My reason told me that instead of sitting there twiddling my thumbs, I should be up and doing some job such as drives away dreaming, protects against temptation and brings oblivion. So I stood up and said:

"I can't get to the town today. But I mustn't sit here idling. Have you got a pick and spade?"

"What do you want them for?"

"To dig that hole."

"Aha! And I thought you just wanted to scare me."

"No. That might have been a bit premature."

"And do you have to do it?"

"Yes. I gave my word to the corpse."

She shook her head. Then she took me off to the lean-to, where several dozen different kinds of rusting tools of every size and shape were piled up higgledy-piggledy. I hauled them out and tidied them up, mild confusion written all over my features.

She watched me for a while with her arms folded.

"Have you ever even used any of them before?"

I liked that, indeed I did. I almost burst out laughing and would have loved to have given her a kiss as reward for her words. But now I needed to look as inscrutable as possible. I grabbed two medium-sized items and set them across my shoulder.

She was watching me, shaking her head.

"You were lying, weren't you?"

Now she had me. I'd given myself away. But how? I was in a quandary, and to conceal the fact I played the even bigger hypocrite.

"Why?"

"You did say you were a gravedigger."

I looked first at her, then at myself. I was wearing only shorts for the summer, a sleeveless shirt and boots. Then it dawned. Even if I were to abandon all my things here with no regrets, even the things that I thought I couldn't die without, I really shouldn't dash off coatless. If only not to be a laughing stock to my friends.

I bowed and said with a smile:

"Don't worry! I won't embarrass the corpse and I'll put a suit on."

"Not that! You'd be sweating before you even got there. It's very hot."

"But I can't go looking like this, can I?"

"Why not?"

"It might be all right here. You won't be offended by it. But there? Who knows who I might meet! And with strangers I ought to look dignified, not like some stripling."

"But it suits you!"

That look! That voice! I'm sure she was only making fun of me, but it hit me in such a way that there could be no further question of glancing back at her, let alone going upstairs to fetch my coat, cap, wallet, watch or even my ID card, so I left without looking back, taking the pick and spade with me.

It was hot and deathlike. Although I was wearing only a shirt, shorts and boots and the way led downhill, the tools soon became as burdensome as that which was wedged in my mind and would not, not for a single instant, stop harrying me.

So what was I actually doing? I'd thought of running away. All right. I really wouldn't have regretted the loss of either my coat, even though it held not only a fair sum of money but also my other essentials, or my rucksack, in which I had placed all my dearest keepsakes, but what was I to say to the kind people to whom I'd bade farewell the previous day and whom I was sure to meet again? Nothing but the honest truth, since any lie would have given itself away sooner than soon. But could I articulate it? The fact that I'd fled in the face of temptation, and so hurriedly that I hadn't even managed to grab my cap and coat? Such an admission might in reality be an act of great courage, but...! As the devil might preach to a whore – what would be the point? I would really rather have abandoned everything, avoided meeting anyone and gone, capless, coatless and on foot and beggarly, straight back to where I had left my better judgement.

Oh, to hell with it –

But then I'd promised her that I'd secure a document allowing her to stay there. What now? Honour is honour and a word given is given.

And then I had a vision of them, shaking their heads and goggle-eyed, as they heard a madman acting on behalf of someone from whom he had himself escaped, without even grabbing his coat and cap. That would be enormously intriguing. They would surely be less bemused by the figure I cut than by my pitiful senility. That I had fled in the face of temptation might have been understandable. But could I have been so weak as to be unable to tell the person concerned the truth, taking my cap and coat and departing with all due decorum?

Yes. I would have had to say that I was indeed so weak, and that any idea of cosily playing the hermit had been grossly misjudged. And if they were to have had a good laugh at the notion –

Well?

Obviously. Suppose they did have a good laugh and suppose word of my folly spread far and wide, would that not be better than what would have followed had I stayed on there?

But this was bad, and I began to have a good laugh at my own expense:

"I did warn you! Wasn't it the last thing you needed?"

Then I began so to enjoy being laughed at that my jaunt passed as in a dream and in no time I was standing on the steps to the church. And having ascertained that no ghost had been and borne the coffin away, I selected a vacant spot conveniently close to the church door and began to dig.

I didn't pray as I dug: I would scarcely have been so incautious. I couldn't shake off the suspicion that the coffin concealed only the corpse of a dog or goat, but it was surely not down to me to check. It was hot. I took off my shirt, glad of the opportunity to get a tan on my back as I worked. The sight of me was anything but edifying, but the work did go well, and the first time I stopped for a breather I was already knee-deep in the hole that I'd dug. Then it got harder and harder, and I was only thigh-deep in the hole when I took a second rest, at which point I began to worry in case I developed blisters that would render further work impossible. But I soon got back into the swing of things, especially once I hit a layer of soft, blue-grey clay, which exuded a heavy, raw coolness.

I was standing breast-high in the hole when it became so appealing that I fancied trying it out and lay down in the bottom on my bare, so far only lightly tanned back. But then I couldn't leap up fast enough. It was cold and hipped me like the jaws of a skeleton. So I clambered out of the grave and lay down on a sun-warmed spot at the edge of the shadow cast by the contorted crown of a linden tree.

Having stared long and hard into the opal shades of the cadaverous clay, I could think of nothing more agreeable than to lie with gay abandon in the grass, with the sky above me, the freshly dug hole beside me and the abandoned church, inside which the forgotten coffin rested on its bier, behind me. Not far away to the side where I had dug the grave was the forest, and in the forest the track guarded by a viper, and to the other side lay the hamlet with a forgotten name, where I'd had suddenly revealed to me, and just as suddenly taken from me, my lost paradise. And in the middle of everything the quivering scorpion that was gnawing the inside of my heart.

Meanwhile the sun had moved on, and being without my watch, I couldn't afford to yield to my weariness. The worst job was perhaps not the mere digging of the hole. What about the coffin?

Unquestionably I would have preferred to dredge up from my memory the image of the living being who had red hair, clear blue eyes and a little rose petal on each cheek. But little use that would have been! The rose petals had fallen from my hand. So I entered the church, walked round the bier and gave it a little shove. Well, the jarring inside me was even worse than the jarring in the legs of the rickety bier. I tried to drag it slowly. It worked. It jarred now and again and creaked so savagely as to send a shiver right through me, but now I was tugging it like the very devil towards the main door. Then there was the problem of the step, and the second and the third, and as the bier began to tilt, the coffin shifted so abruptly that some sludge came shooting out of it. And now I had a premonition of how it could drop with a bang, burst open and go plop and of how my eyes and nose would be full of it, and how I would start coughing and sneezing and cursing.

I saw that a little more prudence was called for. I felt sure that with due caution I could have dragged the bier as far as the hole. But how was I to haul the coffin off it? How could it be lowered without coming apart in my hands? I didn't want merely to tip it off. What if it transpired that it did only contain the rotting remains of a dog! I wasn't duty bound to check first before depositing it in hallowed ground. So the dog might lie within it till the day of judgement, then he could bark to his heart's content! But not yet, not today!

I seized the spade and trimmed the narrow end of the grave into an inclined plane down which the coffin could be lowered without jeopardy. That then was one thing. But were I myself to haul the coffin down, I would have to be standing in the grave. So how to make way for it, turn and climb back out of the grave?

First I needed to gauge in advance every essential move, allow room for it and widen the grave with a kind of alcove within which I could stand safely. I was amazed at my own resourcefulness, but things were looking dire and my back was aching and my disquiet only grew as the shadows lengthened and grew cooler. But having done what I deemed necessary, I clambered out of the grave and made for the coffin.

I approached the bier and, having bowed solemnly to whatever lay within the coffin, be it a human corpse or the carcass of a dog, I began slowly, oh so slowly, to lift it rather than pull it down. Whatever was inside the coffin was not entirely indifferent to my consideration. It commenced at once to thank me, responding with the most exquisite manners, quite unusual in the living, and astonishing me with an unrivalled medley of rustling, rattling and squelching sounds and the magnificent foulness of its stench, hitherto not fully appreciated. My main concern, however, was that the coffin should not take charge of its own descent from the bier before I had dragged it over to the hole, and I began per-force to relish the whole proceeding like some child's game.

The more patiently I played with it, the more fun it was. I gradually succeeded in raising the head end of the bier, propping it opposite the grave, hauling the coffin down to the spot prepared for it and nudging it forward so that the foot end hung over the edge of the pit. Then I jumped down and, using both hands, pulled it lovingly towards me. I had got it half-way when I felt it starting to buckle. I reached my hands out under the middle section, squeezed along to its side, and now I was practically holding it in my embrace and clutching it to my heart. All well and good. The base must have had holes in it and something started dripping on my boots. I leaned back against the side of the grave, but my hands and bare back were getting chafed and the thing was quite heavy. I considered pulling it down and letting it slide to the bottom.

That might have seemed simple enough, but a quite unforeseen obstacle presented itself: the wary coffin also had feet, and it wedged one of them on something and declined to enter the grave, apparently preferring to break in two.

What now? I twisted it this way and that and tried pushing it back, but achieved nothing. It was determined not to enter the grave, most definitely not. My arms and legs had started to ache, time was not standing still, and now I was thinking less about the corpse and more about the approach of evening, the approach of darkness, and hoping that someone would lighten the darkness with a candle in a wire holder and would again be mounting those creaking stairs and would again depress the rusting door handle and again stop, trembling –

And lo and behold!

There she was. She'd brought my cap and coat. And I realised at once that all my musing about what I should do and where I should go had only been an irresponsible, beguiling game played by my wicked imagination. It was flattering that she could have come perhaps fearing that even now I might run away. Yet it irked and piqued me. She had caught me unawares and I smarted with mortification.

Meanwhile she had spotted my distress. She set down my cap and coat and squatted down next to the coffin. With a solemn dignity and gravity it then began to rise at the head and travel slowly across my arms and chest. For all my astuteness, I hadn't reckoned with the fact that not all corpses are equally stiff and motionless. And this one had already started to liquefy and slip downwards, shifting its centre of gravity as if desirous of adopting a sitting position. I wanted to move one hand to stop it slipping away or the base snapping. I don't know how I did it, but at that point it happened.

My uninvited assistant's fingers must have slipped upwards to the lower edge of the lid. It popped up, and then my nose tingled, my teeth clicked and clacked and I would much rather have dumped the coffin down, except there was no place to do it, and fearing what might otherwise have followed, I gripped it so tightly and so frantically that it abraded my skin and drew blood. Well, I did hold on and without a single hiss of pain. Through all this I was unsure what to marvel at first, so for now I focused on the raised lid, measuring the gaping angle which it enclosed along with whatever lay within the coffin, and wondering whether I mightn't have to remain standing there in that hole, nursing that coffin, until Domesday. But that wouldn't have been too bad. I was standing in a grave after all. It was a refuge that I'd dug myself. Above me, I would have seen that red, tousled, gleaming hair, the rose-petal features, the fiery lips. I would have been holding the coffin as a wedding gift and quivering with expectancy. She would have been standing over the grave, leaning across, holding the lid in her hand and watching, watching –

However, the coffin was so heavy and I couldn't have held on to it because something inside kept shifting, its edges cut into me and the mouldering wood made my sweat-drenched skin itch horribly, and my powers were ebbing away. I needed to squat, rest the coffin on my knees and take a brief respite. But there was the problem of the lid, not fully detached yet, which was not only obstructive, but also presented a danger to both my stupid nose and my uninvited assistant. This brought me to my senses and I called:

"Drag the lid off and toss it somewhere! But mind you don't fall!"

The nails grated, and it squeaked, sagged and sloshed. Oh, how it slashed and rammed its way into the lungs and veins and sinews! How it fumed in the nose and smouldered in the eyes! Oh, this was refreshment to end all refreshments, with the stenches and aromas of all the sweetnesses of the world, like putrid lilies, and it gladdened the heart even more than shards of glass! But I even neglected to say thank you. I just spluttered and coughed so violently that my very bones seemed to be coughing.

But this was just the toast ahead of a great banquet prepared for the sheerest pleasure of my flesh, which I had myself induced like a mortal sin, albeit unconsummated. But now it dragged me down and I was sinking, propping myself like a concussed squirrel against the side of the grave. My bent back was being showered with soil, the coffin with its corpse was threatening to fall in, gravitating feet first towards terra firma, and there was some leakage and it squelched about me, but then I managed to squat down, get my breath back and with my customary ineptitude jam the opposite side of the rickety coffin against the wall of the grave as well.

I almost felt jubilant. It freed my hunched-up legs and I could stand up, let the coffin down to the bottom of the grave and straighten my back. Oh, the sheer bliss! The sense of satisfaction! I was barely conscious

that what I'd cast loose was a wedding gift, whether for her or for me. But my nose was itching and I suddenly sneezed, at which point, out of concern that I might have woken the corpse, I glanced to see if it really was asleep.

And suddenly I beheld all the beauties of my soul.

They were awesome. They represented all the beatitude of the senses, all the stupor of intoxication, all the magnificence of insanity. They had a human likeness. Only human? But of course! And so true! So perfect! So breathtakingly rudimentary! They had no legs, so they couldn't stand, but they were able to writhe in triumph and elation. And they had no arms or bones or sinews, for all such things would only be a hindrance to their boundless euphoria. And they had no eyes. These had deliquesced about the surface of their blissful bodies, which sensed, through each and any of their parts, only that which diffused delight. And they had no mouth and they were laughing with the luminescent and heart-warming mucilage that exuded from the corpse like love-sweat inviting further libertinism. The sheer numbers of those mystical pupae and grandiose grubs! Those silken, velveteen and fine linen maggots! How they twisted, writhing about and hanging off everything that was inside the coffin fit to make one's lips constrict!

Yet for all my consternation, I cared less about those kindly maggots than about that at which they were gnawing. Initially my eyes were still veiled by disdain for the unfamiliar matter that had been brazenly polluting the church with its smell, but now the scales fell from them, they opened wide and took sober cognizance of the actual state of affairs.

Well, it wasn't a dog. It proved to have clothes, if putrid and tattered, and something that vaguely resembled shoes. The face was already unrecognisable, the mouth had no lips, and the periosteum shone wanly through the splits in the disintegrating skin like clouded opal, and the filthy bits of peel hanging in the abandoned and despondent pits of the empty eye sockets afforded only a refuge to chrysalises, and the whole was oozing and teetering and leaking out of the coffin. You might have thought it would prefer to be sitting on a spade and just lying there, rotting away. But it had hair, and not short hair either.

Aha, a woman! Another one!

At first I was afraid that my patience would give out and I might rip the whole thing apart. It had to be picked up and put back down exactly as it had lain before being moved, and any dirt pushed out of the way, even if only by hand. But it was slippery and if I gripped it with any extra firmness, it stuck to my fingers and elbows and bare chest like soap and lye.

"There's no point glowering," I told myself. "You've got what you asked for!"

I might have given up, but something held me back and I suddenly felt my shame splitting me asunder. Those filthy bits of peel hanging in the ransacked and despondent pits of the empty eyes and affording only a refuge to chrysalises had now spotted me. They stared into my heart and at that moment I'd have gladly exchanged the bulbous and bothersome balls of my own red-hot eyes for something more like those filthy bits of peel, which gazed with greater nobility and saw with greater clarity than that out of which my own gutless sentimentality was peering. Even the defenceless mouth that had no lips was saying something in an inaudible, but beautiful language. And above us the bright, golden-bluish air and the heavy, stupefying magic of old age and death.

I'm certain that the deceased was looking at me as if the connection between her soul and this body had not been broken completely. But what did she really want? Had she truly been distressed by the beauty of a golden day and the remembrance of what she had failed to achieve in life and what might not even be on the Other Side? Was she begging for consolation? Or could it have been she who was trying to console me?

But what was that protruding there, stranded at the coffin's foot? A dog after all?

Oh, power! Oh, majesty! Oh, wisdom of God! Look, a baby! Ah! It was hunched down there like a sin denied, already beginning to disintegrate and decay and lose its limbs and it was only with the greatest care that I could take it up into my arms.

"Bother," I groused, "as if one corpse weren't enough! Why should it have fallen to me of all people to be burying two at once!"

But then I registered that the thing that had once been a child, now, even in the embrace of death, turning its eyes only towards its mother, was lying so easily in my embrace, quivering more with fear than love, that I was uncertain whether I shouldn't turn it towards me in such a way that it would have my heart next to its hungry mouth and could taste the blood from my freshly grazed skin. So I tried turning it towards me and I was gasping for air and I looked anxiously and sidelong for the mysterious mother. But the child didn't wake. So what was I to do? Just lay it down, make the sign of the cross over it, cover it with the coffin lid, then clamber out and shovel the soil back.

One last look at that defenceless mouth that had no lips, at the clouded opal of the wanly shining periosteum, at the filthy strips of peel in the empty eye-sockets now affording a refuge only to chrysalises, and at that which had once been a baby. It was not a farewell taken easily of course. Oh, my heart! Enough now!

Having climbed out of the hole, I could do nothing but rush across to the pump and wipe away the sticky ooze and slimy maggots, and I offered no resistance when my uninvited assistant began to rub and scrub me like a wicked stepmother, since even I myself was ashamed of the revolting state I was in. Then I jumped up, shook myself down and stretched. The sun was still ablaze and I felt ecstatic. But quickly, whether from fear of catching cold, or, more likely, lest she saw the abrasions on my elbows and chest and started nagging at me, I cocooned myself in my shirt, sat down on the grave and said:

"I thought you'd never show up!"

I can't say who had prompted me. I'm sure I meant it to be a downright lie, but it was true.

"I'm really sorry! I didn't know you were in such a hurry."

"Come and sit down!"

She sat down.

"Not like that! Opposite me!"

"And where am I supposed to put my legs?"

"Ah legs! Well... How about here, between mine. Yes, like that! And your hands in your lap!"

I gripped her between my knees. She stared at me and her eyes filled with venom. And the more venomous they grew, the more acutely I sensed my own weakness by comparison.

"Did you know I was thinking of disappearing?"

"Yes. How could I not know? I do have eyes. And now?"

"I can't go now."

"Why not?"

"What would the viper say?"

"Ah! That beast! Are you afraid of it? Is it worse than me?"

"I really couldn't say. But it doesn't matter now. The only place I can die is here."

"Why so?"

"My mind's made up."

"But what else do you want?"

"Please stop worrying. Just look at that glorious sky! It wants to hear your voice, so you must cherish what you can say before you die! Think of the dead woman here in the grave. How gladly she would have spoken!"

"I'm not sure what's got into –"

"Start talking!"

"What about?"

"About how you coped."

Her cheeks flared red-hot.

"Must I?"

"I think you know."

"But it will be horrible."

"All the better."

"All right. I'd better begin with the window pane. I myself was standing a little way off by the exit, where there were no windows, and before I realised I could jump through the window as well, before I could catch my breath and make a move, the way was blocked. And I can still hear the sound today. That's the most terrible thing about it. It will never pass. Shame's one thing. Hm! Shame! But the envy!"

"I know. I expect she was beautiful."

"Maybe. She wasn't local and I didn't even know her. She only came here to die."

"Don't tell me. Instead of you. Only that made it worse for you."

"Yes. After that I couldn't do it. I know I staggered, and I seemed to be falling, falling, I heard the sound of glass shattering and could feel glass in my throat. And someone was rubbing against me, crushing me, spread-eagling me, and when he let me go all I wanted was for him to stamp on me and trample me to nothing. As you see, he didn't. Then another one came. Sure,

I hissed about getting my own back, but he just laughed.
Then a third came, and by then I felt so strange, alien,
as if I wasn't me at all. Well, so many of them came that
by the next day I couldn't even move. I lay on my front,
face to the ground, but I wasn't in a stupor, I was still
seething and couldn't even see how ridiculous it all was.
Meanwhile the other girls had at least had a good cry

and were worrying in case they fell pregnant. I was the only one incapable of having a good cry. That was the worst thing. So it's been locked inside me ever since."

"It's good you didn't cry."

"Hah! It's all very well for you to say that! It took me all night, a whole terrible night and all the following day before I fully understood that it was too late for anything. And then I would have loved to have a good cry, if only for not having dived headlong at the window pane instead. The other girls would doubtless have fully made up for that omission, perhaps gladly. They'd had their cry and got used to the idea by then. Only then did it begin to go on at me: Well? Are you satisfied? Do you know how many consorts you've had? Have you been counting them? Or are you still minded to leap at the window? Then I raised myself up and calculated the jump I'd need to take, but at that point I realised I'd left it too late. Even for dying. And honour? Hardly! That was gone. Both for here and in the eternal life. There too, instead of blood and tears in my eyes and veins, I shall only ever feel splinters of glass. But honour? Hardly!"

Her voice sounded as sweet as an Angelus bell from the other side of the hills. Just to kneel and hearken to the sounds was all it would have taken. But I wanted to see her and something was blocking my view. Those splinters of glass were poking from her eyes and preventing me from seeing into them as I needed to. And although I was jealous of them, with their pointed ends holding my will in check like powerless dust, it was quite futile, since what loomed from them was but a splintered and ruptured picture of that fiercely determined virgin who had desired to fall headlong against window glass rather than jeopardise her honour for a single second. But then the picture and all its splinters began to rise and grow like a stained-glass window, its disparate parts joined into one not by strips of lead, but by blackened blood and tears of frost, and the coldly venomous and insensitive glinting of all the elongated and jagged edges, the stunted points of glass and the cracks in it suddenly began to form a curious spectral halo, which was so cumbersome that the head couldn't sustain it and kept falling limply out of the picture, face, nape and neck.

The picture even had a frame. It was the frame of that first-floor window that faced due south and was surely so welcoming that the random beholder could scarcely have told that death had laid its miscreant trap in it. For all that, the virgin's head kept falling out of the picture, down to the bottom edge of the frame as to the edge of a bier, and the fugitive, ruptured reflection of her face was caught only in splinters of glass.

Certainly there was no beauty left in the face. It was swollen. Its attitude was like that of a hanged man with the knot in the middle of his neck. And her youthful forehead no longer invited a kiss, for the last convulsion before death had puckered it into several deep wrinkles, and the constricted face was of such repellent aspect that one's bones fidgeted.

However, it being turned down to face the ground or the parapet below the window, down which blood trickled, if I had wanted to view it not more at my ease, but in such a way as to take in properly that which could not display its likeness other than in an unnatural position and inverse direction, like a cast-down statue or felled tree, I would have to have been either hanging or standing head-down and to have twisted myself in a particular way so as to see what I was observing above me the right way up. I am sure it would have been best for me if I'd been able, by whatever means, to have found myself beneath that being just as she hurled herself from the window, to have been facing towards her, and then, lying on my back among the splinters as they jabbed me in my perverse neck, I could have had her fiercely determined face before my eyes and swallowed her last breath along with the blood. Then the image would have been both purer and more natural. But for now I had to forego that until the day when I would definitely see her somewhere in the next world, though from some remote corners of my memory an image of something more definite was emerging instead.

Thus does a baby leave its mother's womb as it labours in the final convulsion. It too falls headlong and swollen-faced into the vile trap that death snaps shut. But from what accursed and appalling womb had the fierce virgin in the picture been struggling free? What convulsion had so propelled her that she had dashed herself, dashed, like a crazed bird head-first into the glass?

Aha! Now I understood. The sky back then had been so beautiful! Just like now. How powerful its beckoning to faraway places, places endless and magnificent! What was there here? Away, away! And fear not to fly! No hanging about, hopping up and down and stretching one's wings, but fly, through a window, up a chimney, or ventilation shaft, or along a sewer if it came to it, and have no dealings with death! And should the window be closed, do not stop, smash through the glass and fly, for whoso is true shall surely outwit death!

That was the image of the dead woman. And I would have compared it to the image of this one who was alive as if it could be different from the one that loomed from the splinters of glass, but by now I couldn't distinguish between them. In vain would I have asked which one

had swallowed which, since they had now taken up residence in a single body. And I saw the head, so heavy that it resembled that of a baby terror-stricken by the convulsion of the mother giving it birth, and the spikes of the splinters, whose chilling glint formed a curious spectral halo round the head, and the red hair that luminesced at the temples as in the half-light floating around a lamp on a tombstone, and the rose petals and the involuntarily parted and contorted lips. And the envy! And the envy! For sure, the living one was but the coffin of the dead one, who had found liberation, but could not decompose. And on her head she also had to wear a halo that was not hers and was a constant reminder to her that it hadn't been she who had outwitted death. And she couldn't cry. Instead of tears in her eyes she had just splinters of glass. And because of the splinters projecting also from her throat she could neither cry out, nor turn her face aside. So this was that defiance, that sneer, that disdain, that rancour, that beauty! Ah –

My heart lurched. Only now did I recognise how empty and paltry my entire life would have been were it not for her.

"It's a good thing you didn't manage to catch your breath in time!"

"Why? What's it to you?"

"It's not me who matters now. The main thing's you."

"Aha! So now I'm the main thing!"

She stood up. She was shaking. She might have been about to escape my grasp and leave. But with nowhere to go! It was too late now. My legs impeded her. Then she glanced up, snubbing the thing that was me as something accursed, up towards the sky.

I could neither release her, nor stand up. Our legs hampered us and I could only look at her from below. She was standing over me, her face as in ecstasy, pale, majestically grave and inclined wistfully to the left. And suddenly I felt how high, so very high, she was above me, how dusk was gathering about me and night beginning to fall.

"Stand still! Please stand still! As if on a marble column! As if clad in gold! There! Now that's you!"

Hearing this took her aback and she immediately sat down. But it was too late. It had sufficed. I had glimpsed her true countenance. Doubtless she was seeing her mother. But meanwhile she had replied:

"You should have seen into me back then."

"Why?"

"Inside me there was this hooting and jeering and wriggling and laughing, then it fell silent for a moment, and suddenly everything seemed different."

"And the men?"

"Oh yes! That's the point!"

"And afterwards?"

"Why do you ask?"

"It was you who said I should have seen it."

"And do you want to?"

"Of course."

"Well I hope you enjoy it! It can't really matter what horrors assailed me. It was nothing. I came out of the worst blackout and then – But you know what it's like!"

"But you mustn't spare yourself now!"

Things were coming to a head. She looked at me as at a vicious dog, but then lowered her head and may not even have sensed herself touching my lips with a lock of her hair. My breath was bated and my mouth was full of her. That red hair began to quiver and in doing so inscribed on my lips even the minutest tremor of her most adorable voice.

"While I was still seething with rage and a desire for revenge, my anger, pathetic as it was, was some safeguard against drowning. But then the main thing came. By then I was so stupefied that I wouldn't have been able to think about anything, or want anything, or even move once my rigid body had sensed, beneath the weight, that it wasn't too bad if I just let go –"

Her voice, which had been quavering with bashfulness, began to falter. Then suddenly something inside her rose up. She lifted her head, looked at me and her eyes spat sparks like a blacksmith's forge.

So the bashful anguish had been but a ruse. So much the better. If there was to be a duel, then be it complete with every subterfuge! The blow had struck home. I stiffened my resolve and, wearing the most innocent expression I could muster, launched my own attack.

"How often? Just the once?"

"No. It happened again."

"Every time?"

She glanced at me, but without a hint of blushing, as she blurted:

"No! Actually, no! Only sometimes."

"I knew it."

Her cheeks turned scarlet.

"How did you know, if you don't mind?"

"It's obvious. I can hear your voice and I'm watching you. Do go on."

"No. That's it."

"Really? Why not? Are you ashamed at being only a woman? I don't think so! What's a man? The only difference is that the most insignificant of men is always powerful enough to get the better of the devil. If the going gets tough, he can, even at the last second, bite his tongue, or just one lip even, and it's all over. The devil has to retire empty-handed. In such dire straits even a woman would gladly bite her tongue or split her lip. But where would that get her? Nowhere. Nowhere at all. It wouldn't help stop anything. Is it not the case that even dead women get raped?"

"I know. But all that is no excuse."

"Meaning?"

"If I'd at least split my lip, I'm sure the pain would have stopped me feeling the very thing that took away my sense of shame."

"Aha! You can't know that. That's a thing you can try once only, and then it's done with. It doesn't get repeated. That's what a gag's for. And isn't it a blessing that at the very moment when the body feels about to dry up and burn away, its very burns are suddenly visited by a sensual thrill like some delectable drug as recompense for all the suffering? And why resist it? After all, the sin wasn't yours."

She compressed her lips, jerked her neck and replied with a grimace:

"Well I'll be...! So the loss of one's modesty and honour isn't something to be ashamed of now, but a peculiar kind of blessing!"

"And how would you have it?"

"Is the soul a louse? Is it so wretched, so squalid as to be genuinely capable of accepting such a blessing?"

Each of the words' constituent sounds landed on my lips like a kiss of beatification and my eyelashes bowed down, unable to withstand the impact of the sparks that glittered and died, which were as intimidating as they were beseeching, which were imploring as they held back all the magnificence of the tears that were waiting for the loveliest and purest moment. Even any unseen beings were probably holding their breath, transfixed in rapture. I alone kept on and on, harassing her more remorselessly than any hound back into that hell where they had surely tormented her less vilely than I was tormenting her now.

"Why mightn't it? Look here! I know what a sense of shame is, but a body's a body and we know what it wants. So why make a secret of it? I'll be blunt: Imagine if your heels hadn't got a purchase of their own accord – I'm right, aren't I? And the soul? Well, what about it? It has to know what life's like!"

"Can you really be so nasty?"

"Why so? What *is* life? Knocks, kicks, stonings and getting spat on. That's the main thing, and the only place to find glory and honour. So, should we accept it? We have no other option! No. Of course we don't want to, but if we did, would it really be what it's meant to be?"

"Even the shame that I have to bear now?"

"And where *is* the shame?"

I was as much compelled to ask as she was to respond, for about us stood a host of invisible beings and it was all set up like a trial after death. But who was it trying her? Or who might still be entitled to ask her things? Only her mother might. But not even she was sitting in judgement over her, nor questioning her about anything, though she had taken her with her on her final journey and died in her stead. The invisible beings had only been there as witnesses. They hadn't dared to ask questions, lest they prematurely drive from her doleful eyes the awesome, immortal and beautiful expression with which, at the gravest moment of her violation, she looked upon the dignified dying of her wordless mother. To her alone she turned as she was being torn asunder with shame. To her alone she was confiding her anguish before replying. To her alone she was complaining of being stifled by remorse. Oh, this was no trial! But what then? What?

She could now reply to my question with absolute resignation:

"It's in my subsequent acceptance of those things, so passive that even if I were to have begun coughing up blood, I wouldn't have found the resolve to bite through my tongue."

"Really? And what did that make you? A measly worm on a fisherman's hook? Even a worm will at least give an involuntary twitch if tickled. And you can't hold its inability to detach itself from the hook against it!"

Her lips parted, but she said nothing. All I could detect was her heaving breath, and all I could see in her eyes was the kind of sorrowful glint that accompanies a song as it fades into the distance. Meanwhile she was watching me like a star that returns day after day to its window of choice and waits and waits.

But there was still the grave and it was getting quite late.

"Well? Is that all?"

"I think so. At least the nastiest bit."

"So let's finish the job. Shovel the soil back over it. But let's say a prayer first."

I stood up. I bent my head, then she rose and made to leave.

But now? What prayer? The battle still wasn't won. We were still standing facing each other. What should I do about her? I would certainly have liked her to join me in reciting aloud the words of a prayer, but then it struck me that she wouldn't be up to saying any other words than those she had used to her mother: "Come and watch, if you want, and do it instead of me! –"

Ah! Those words would surely be the sincerest of all. They rang with the pain of love and the muteness of tears. They rang with the desperation of shame and the trickling of blood. Their beauty brought tears to the eyes and their sweetness could induce insanity. So better not, then, for now!

And I began to declaim:

"In nomine Patris –"

I made no assumption that she would understand the Latin, but I was in no doubt that she knew what it was, and that she would be incapable of opposing the mode I'd chosen.

"Pater noster –"

But suddenly I was at a loss and began vainly reflecting on the meaning of those opening words. We weren't siblings, were we? Or wedded into one? Were we really alone now in the entire world? Just she and I? What should I reply were I to be asked what we were?

My voice grew sluggish. I went on slowly, very slowly, ever more slowly and diffidently.

"Sanctificetur nomen tuum –"

The earth started to heave beneath my feet and I began to feel dizzy. The words were no longer issuing from my own cognizance, my own will, my own mouth, but from all that surrounded us, me and her, now as before.

"Fiat voluntas tua –"

Ah, that title deed! That window pane! And those eyes!

It was all dancing before my eyes. As if by unseen forces her skulking consorts were being dragged by the shoulder out of their enchanted holes and I saw their gaping and popping eyes, dull, unseeing and uncomprehending, and the tacky smirk on their sleazy lips. They were positioned standing or seated or raised up towards her like monsters who spent their nights in the dark of an ice-cold cavern and had been blinded by

fire and stupefied by smoke, and she stood there lost in
ecstasy, her head raised heavenwards and half-turned,
like back then, to the side from which she could see her
mother. Ah –

"Sicut in coelo –"

I'm sure I then seemed to be seeing a picture of her
in the Book of Life, raised in glory on an elevation.
And I? What was I looking for here? What did I want?

"Panem nostrum –"

What comes next? Aha. This:

"quotidianum –"

But haven't we died? Am I really supposed to stay here with her, break bread with her, share a household with her, and a grave? And why am I shaking like this? What is this shrieking inside me so loud that my lips are repeating it?

"Da nobis –"

Oh! Might it even be actually possible? She, staring at me out of the Book of Life, not comprehending her real glory, and I? What am I? But I'm blaspheming. Going mad. What am I wishing upon myself?

"Et dimitte nobis –"

But who is to be forgiven and for what? Could well be me after all. But surely not in advance? But what exactly? What? Surely not –"

"debita nostra –"

My blood began to run cold and I saw the grave and my own heart. And something began to fall silent, until it fell totally silent, but then came the words:

"Et ne nos inducas –"

Let it hurt! Who cares! I've got what I wanted. The pinnacle of desire before my eyes, a gulf on every side, and a scorpion in my heart – Ah!

"Ave –"

Slowly now! Slower! And no sobbing!

"Ora pro nobis peccatoribus nunc et in hora mortis –"

Go on, say it!

" – nostrae."

And now say: "Amen!"

I willed myself to start reciting the prayer for the dead as well. But by then I was in no mind to stop. No, no mind. I was in no hurry. For now I was at least saved. And the scorpion?

Let him wait!

I remembered the prayer with which the souls of the dying are accompanied to the other side and with which I wanted to take leave of myself forever.

"Salve, Regina –"

I'm sure she knew the first two words at least, for she bowed her head and her clasped hands tightened even further.

"Mater misericordiae –"

I faltered.

"Vita dulcedo –"

It seemed unlikely I'd be able to finish the prayer. But I wasn't giving up just yet –

"– et spes nostra –"

I was fighting hard to stay in control, pausing for breath, then going on again, until I sobbed:

"O Virgo –"

At that point my throat tightened and I was seized with shaking, and tears came streaming from my eyes and, wishing her not to see into my face, I fell at her feet and put my arms around her ankles and burst out sobbing and, practically breathless, I began to kiss her shoes, filthy though they were with dust and trampled clay. And I kept kissing the shoes, again and again, wiping the dust from them with my quavering lips, and I didn't hear what she was saying and ignored her efforts to stop me, and I might never, never have let go had she not stooped herself and knelt down beside me.

When I finally rose to my feet, my face was covered in drying tears and soil and clay, but I ignored all that and immediately set about the task at hand. She helped. When I finished piling the soil on top of the grave, she herself grabbed the bier and hauled it back into the church. I sprinkled the pool left by the corpse with sand, meaning to clean it up properly later. Then we gathered up our tools, slung them over our shoulders and left.

In the gaps in the tops of the contorted linden trees dazzling sparks from the setting sun flickered, the shadows were cool now, and we spoke not a single word.

We set off. The church and graveyard soon disappeared behind us, as if they had sunk into the past. I wanted to think. I felt that I ought to. But something was stopping me. I would have liked to think in order not to see, but it wasn't vouchsafed to me to think and I had to see. By then I'd stepped out of the invisible and enchanted circle and lost my bearings. And my feet were sore, but I had to keep going and I couldn't even console myself with the prospect of a rest.

I recalled how, the previous evening, I'd looked up at the church, which I'd seen in the glare of the setting sun as an ancient, reliable and exalted landmark. I recalled being drawn towards it, hurrying up to its doorway, how I'd carelessly grasped the handle, and how it had opened so unexpectedly easily and quickly that I might have stumbled had I not been holding the handle firmly in my grasp. And how inside I'd seen nothing but shadows and cobwebs and the extinguished sanctuary lamp. And yet it hadn't been as desolate and empty as it seemed, since there had been that bier with the black coffin, with something oozing out of it and forming a pool on the floor, dried round the edges, but with a trickle snaking out of it towards the door. So it was here that I had entered the enchanted circle from which there was no return.

What had I done? I'd hauled the coffin out of the church, dug a grave, buried the coffin in it and finally sprinkled the pool with sand. And now I was walking away, unwilling to look back to see if someone might be running after me and threatening me and shouting that I had stolen the coffin, the property of the church as its last, unappreciated and sole treasure, and that I should return it. But now I had no desire to render it up, not even if the entire landscape had started to threaten me and the hills to shake and wail fit to make me shrivel with fear.

We walked on. I wasn't alone and I no longer needed to think about a bed for the night or a place to rest, but my feet were sore, though in quite a different way from the day before. And it wasn't due solely to having dug that pit, and if there was anything at all by way of consolation, it was that my back also ached, for now I would have wished to be aching all over.

As I walked, I feared to glance at the mysterious being who wore, unwitting, the golden crown of glory and from whom I would gladly have bought the shame that she bore, fearing it as she might fear a rigid snake, so that I might share her burden at least as far as my strength permitted. But I possessed nothing with which to pay for it right then. And she might not even have been able to sell it to me. Maybe it had become indivisible. Without the shame there would be no glory.

Yet might not some miracle happen?

But what miracle? That she might stand before me on the plinth of her mystical solitariness in the middle of a derelict church surrounded by the mute, ossified, but eternal witnesses of her harrowing glory, with me at her feet? Like what? Like a dog struck dumb with terror and unable to stir? Yes. That would do. I felt it. And why? Was I hoping to crush the scorpion underfoot? But a scorpion is indestructible.

Oh, I would have liked to think in order not to see, but it was not vouchsafed to me to think and I had to see. And I saw dust and the thirsting glow fading silently beneath my feet, and overhead clouds, replete with blood and darkness, and ahead of me glinted fallen veils of light among the shrouds of shadows, and only on the slope enclosed by two panhandles of woodland did something disturb the calm of my feverish torpidity and deathly thirst. And I wished not so see, but I had to see even the hay cart, which might have seemed entirely lacking in interest were it not for the pair of horses pawing the ground in front.

What's this?

I couldn't believe it, and it irked me to the point of acrimony. Did anyone else have any claim to be here besides us two?

Whether they did or not, someone *was* here. He was holding a pitchfork. And he wasn't alone. There were also some women standing by the cart. Yes, three. That irked me. But how to be rid of them? I had wanted to see but a wasteland and the spectres of dreams. And now?

I would gladly have summoned the devil himself to my aid. But meanwhile the four people had finished their work and were making ready to leave for home not in our direction, but to the far side of the woods, and suddenly everything went topsy-turvy and got jammed inside my head, and whether I realised what I actually meant to do and whom I was breaking faith with thereby, or whether it was impelling me forward as hope propels a drowning man, I stretched out my neck and began calling for help, believing it to be close at hand. Of course my sense of shame was snapping at me and hopping up and down, and of course I couldn't fail to notice that she who was walking beside me as witness and observing in consternation the violent fit of my cowardice, had suddenly begun to tremble and refused to go on, but that came too late to hold me in check.

"Don't be afraid," I tried to soothe her, "let's go over to them! The sooner you get to know them, the better it will be for you too."

I grabbed her hand and dragged her to the footpath that led that way. However, the man by the cart gave not the slightest sign of any interest in us, indeed it rather seemed that he had merely gripped his pitchfork more tightly.

"Oh dear," I said, "they're afraid of us! So let's leave our tools here."

We tossed our pick and spade aside. The man was no dullard. He at once put his pitchfork down. I greeted him from a distance as loudly as possible and showed him that I had nothing in my hands.

He was watching us and at first it struck me that having us for neighbours was far less agreeable to him than having him was agreeable to us. I have no idea what he suspected us of, but I didn't care anyway. Then it struck me that he was less interested in whether I was carrying anything than in my calf-length shorts, which – with the grass already exhaling the heavy cool of evening and my knees turning blue, and possibly even shaking – gave my appearance neither the requisite appeal nor a proportionate magnificence. In that regard I had failed. He didn't even try to disguise his smirk. But what of it! I was glad that the shorts had sparked his sincere interest.

Behind him, by the wagon, stood a woman, somewhat careworn, but by no means lustreless, and a girl of around fifteen. Each was holding a rake and they were looking at me half-agape. But they seemed *not* to be interested in my shorts. Their eyes were directed higher up. Another little girl, who I'd guess was about ten or so, had clambered onto the cart and was peeping at me, some impish idea making the corners of her mouth twitch.

So this was for real. It wasn't a dream, but a genuine way out of my vicious circle. So I repeated my greeting and said:

"I'm glad to see you. Things are going to be jollier from now on."

He parted his lips slightly and said – perhaps only to avoid the impression that he couldn't speak:

"And do you feel sad here?"

"But there are four of you, and only two of us."

"It's only a matter of time."

He half-turned to look at his wife and added:

"As it was for us."

Well, that was one-up to him! I was disconcerted. His tanned features with their first shallow lines and the enduringly shy expression of a young man spoke all too clearly of both his honesty and his reserve. The moment was scarcely right for starting an argument.

Yet he may not have been entirely sure of his prognosis, since now he changed the subject.

"Where did you spring from?"

"God alone knows."

"Have you been here long?"

"No. Only since yesterday."

"And do you want to stay?"

"I wish I knew."

"Are you a farmer?"

"No."

"Of course not. You certainly don't look like one. A tradesman of some kind?"

"Not that either."

"Shopkeeper?"

"Not likely!"

"And what do you mean to do?"

"Nothing. I'm too old."

"Well, I can see you haven't been idle. I expect you've been digging up treasure."

Ha, now he'd shown his hand.

"No," I said, "burying one."

He started and cast an eye towards his pitchfork. But it was out of reach. Then with arms akimbo I looked appreciatively at the pitchfork and began to chaff him:

"And guess where it was!"

He looked at me as at a vicious dog, but said nothing.

"Here in the church. Didn't you know about it?"

He was utterly confused and limited his revenge to a scornful inspection of my shorts.

I went on with my wicked address.

"I've only been here since yesterday, and as I was passing my legs were already aching and I felt like taking a rest in the church. But it was dark inside and there was a funny smell. I didn't like it, but never mind! I went to take a closer look, and that put paid to the idea of resting."

"And now you're worried?"

"About the treasure? Oh, no. That doesn't bother me. It can stay where it is."

"Is it heavy?"

"No," I said, ignoring his rising distrust, for the eyes of my soul suddenly registered her who had already said everything, "it wasn't so much heavy as unwieldy. We could hardly line it up properly."

What we hadn't been able to line up was obviously a bit vague to me too. But the local ploughed on:

"Could it have contained something you didn't want to see?"

"Who's to say. It was reeking and we were afraid in case it all came apart. The bottom was already rotten."

At this point his impatience got the better of him and he looked me straight in the eye:

"And what was it that –"

He didn't finish. He'd meant to ask what had caused the smell, but what he spotted in my expression pulled him up short, leaving him agog and transfixed.

I didn't know what had so terrified him, and out of curiosity I turned towards his wife and daughters. They seemed unable to tear their eyes away from me and I could tell that what so amazed them wasn't the manner of my speaking, but some visible, if not indelible mark, whether on my forehead, lips or my entire face. Now not even the little girl was making fun of me. No. She'd got past that.

I myself might have found it no less strange, but it suddenly dawned: my cheeks were all smeared with dust, wet from tears and the saliva that had trickled from my sobbing lips as I pressed them frantically to those shoes. I'd forgotten to wipe myself clean. So that was the first cause of the child's laughter, and now the smudges must have begun to scare her. Dusk had already descended. I stood facing the setting sun and my countenance, capturing as in a mirror all that was scary about the fading, darkening sky, and branded by those smudges, resembled that of a corpse on a pyre. And I did want to wipe my face, but had no pocket mirror about my person, and loath to daub myself into an even more comical demeanour, I turned with a tacit, yet unmistakable appeal to the woman I had brought to the spot with me.

She was standing close by. She understood my bashful appeal, but she made no move. And the look on her face! There could be nothing more beatific, more overweening, nothing sweeter. She'd been watching the man and the women, but most of all me, or rather the smudges that were unremitting testimony to my having fallen down before her and to what I did next, and she wasn't going to wipe them away, not for anything in the world. And she could see that the women were watching her likewise and guessing, yes trying to guess – well, they were women when all's said and done, and how could they fail to guess right in the end! Women guess everything right. And I was starting to enjoy it and might well have revelled in it, but –

Where was I?

Oh, yes.

I turned towards the man and actually had a brief moment of lucidity. My almost inexplicably grubby face and the fact that I'd confessed to finding treasure in the church and to having set out to retrieve it not only with all the paraphernalia of a seasoned robber, but also with an accomplice, justifiably stirred in him sundry rather gloomy imaginings, which I of course found flattering, given that they served only to inflate my questionable dauntlessness. But did they really inflate it? Couldn't those honest, truthful and sincere eyes see to the very bottom of my soul much better than I?

I would scarcely have laid a hand on money or jewels or other items of value. But was it quite so certain that my eyes hadn't revealed how my blood was in ferment and how my soul couldn't wait for the dark moment when I would commit the even graver and more execrable sacrilege of touching her whom all the powers of heaven had been shielding from me? I could be certain that she wouldn't have opposed me of her own will. That look in her eyes! She was no longer looking to her worthy mother. Now she saw only me. So who should protect her now? Me? Not likely!

My only hope now lay with these people. I turned to the man and said:

"Where did the stench come from? You still don't know?"

"No."

"A dead woman and child. And you couldn't have asked them not to stink. The bodies were already decayed. Do you mean you didn't know anything about it?"

"No. The church has been falling into disrepair for several years now. These days we have to attend the church in town."

"On foot?"

"No. We take the horses. And if you'd like –"

I leapt at the idea.

"Oh, I'd like to very much! I've got some things to do there and I ought to have a word with the parish priest."

"When? Tomorrow?"

I wasn't expecting that and I felt like one who has just been rescued from burning to death. Why so soon? Why now, when everything was so wonderful?

But something jolted me. I don't know whether it was defiance at my own hypocrisy, a sudden flush of vanity, a glimmer of hope of escaping, or merely a frantic bet that moved me to reply:

"All right. When? First thing?"

Well, I might have been acting light-heartedly, but I felt a bit dizzy. And to crown it all, that good man suddenly said:

"You'll be taking your wife with you, right? We can't have her being frightened out here on her own!"

That came as a shock and I began to prevaricate.

"What would she be frightened of?"

"Where do you live?"

"Why?"

"So I know where to come."

"Don't worry. I wouldn't want to put you to the trouble. I'll come to your place."

"Not likely!" his wife cried disapprovingly. "Why you? He's much younger and you're worn ragged from all that work."

"So come with us now," said the man, "right now! Come and sit on the cart. We've got plenty of room at home and you'll be able to have an extra half-hour's lie-in."

This was bad. I was standing in the presence of five people as before five witnesses. And I was the sixth. At that instant I had a sight of myself such as I would never have again. So? Did I want it? Or not? Had I forgotten why I had called out to the man? So why the sudden uncertainty? It was now or never!

But my heart was having twinges of pain and the scorpion was laughing at me. I was at my wit's end and the devil alone came up with a helpful prompt:

"I can't go into town looking like this. I've got official business to see to."

I didn't want to bite my tongue. There might have been only a moiety of truth in each of my words, but I was in no condition to escape the rift in and obscuration of my soul.

Our neighbour seemed to find that my argument carried some weight.

"All right. Should I come round at six, or seven?"

"Whatever suits you."

Oh, those shorts! I now extolled them as the cause of my having gained some time in which to put off making my decision. What a boon it is if, at such a crucial moment, a wise man looks like a scarecrow.

Our neighbour's face brightened and, in an attempt to remedy his previous mistrust, he said as if in jest:

"Sorry, you had me worried. When you started shouting, I mistook you for a burglar. But as you came closer, erm, forgive me –"

"You thought you were seeing a lunatic."

The man shook his head.

"That's not the whole of it. If I'd been seeing a lunatic, I wouldn't have been all that surprised. There's been no shortage of such hereabouts. But who *are* you?"

"Perhaps a burglar after all."

"No, you don't look at all like one now."

"Thank you kindly!"

He smiled.

"No offence! Truly. But why are you here?"

"Dear me! If they could talk, you might get an answer from my poor legs. For my part, I just don't know."

Who's to say if I did or didn't know? But the man's wife knew. She said:

"That's it! It looked to me as if someone was prodding you along like a lame bull. You're depressed about something."

There was beauty in her penetrating gaze.

"I'm senile."

It might have been nothing. No actual word, just a hiss. But it sufficed. She smiled. It was all clear to her.

But her husband wasn't giving up and he began asking more questions:

"And what do you have in mind?"

That might even have been an admonition or warning against some peril. But I found it merely a bit annoying, and before I knew it, I'd come out with:

"To seek my fortune."

"You? Here? Never! You're having me on! Can't you see this place has had it?"

Probably no one could have said anything more sensible if I weren't already so far gone that not only had I thrown caution to the wind, but actually was minded to start an argument, and so that my argument might be the more genuine, I turned to his daughters.

The fifteen-year-old had a most pure, tender and pleasing face, perhaps already a little melancholic and grave. The ten-year-old, while she said nothing, just narrowing her wily eyes the way children do, was a ball of fire and tempest. As I stared at the elder girl, something suddenly jabbed me as if to gain my attention and I turned to look at the woman who had declined to wipe the smudges from my face, and I couldn't fail to see how wistfully she was watching that innocent, pure and beatific face and biting her lip.

"Oh well," I said to our neighbour, "no matter if it has had it, I'm glad that you're here."

"Why?"

"Just look at your wife. Well? You don't need me to tell you how lucky you are. You can see for yourself. And your daughters. The elder one is like a rose on an altar. But mind you don't get too close while you're looking! And the younger one? Ah! See? Do you see? She's got a living squirrel in each eye!"

The squirrels tittered gaily, the rose on the altar turned away shyly, and their mother blushed. Only the father was ill at ease.

"But forgive me," I began excusing myself, "for standing here and going on! It'll be dark soon and your horses are getting restless. You know about us for now –"

"But I don't know who you are and where to find you."

"Over that way," I said, pointing northwards. "Stop just before the path to the cemetery. From there it's better to continue on foot because you won't be able to see it from the cart. Go right, across the footbridge, up the slope –"

The man stared wide-eyed.

"How come you aren't scared, living there all alone?"

"Why? There are two of us. And we have a goat. The house is on two floors and we've got a yard."

He listened ever more attentively and looked ever more astonished. Then he said:

"Did you bring the lady with you?"

"No. She was here already. She got here before me."

"Alone?"

"With the goat."

"And she wasn't afraid?"

"That didn't come into it. She loaded up her things and came."

"That end's been giving me the creeps for ten years. If it weren't for you, I wouldn't go near it even now. And I'm a bloke."

"Why? Is it haunted or something?"

"I know what I've heard, and that's enough for me. I couldn't but be surprised that the lady wasn't afraid to come."

I was standing erect. I knew what he meant. But inside me and all about me everything suddenly began to whirl like a merry-go-round, and although I felt slightly sick I was looking forward to seeing the world from another aspect. So I said:

"That's what I like about it."

He puckered his brow as he turned to look self-consciously at the person he called 'the lady', sensing that it would be polite to say a few words to her too. He probably knew what he meant to say, but as he looked at her he still couldn't pluck up the courage. Instead he put the question to me:

"Did she know the place before?"

"She was even born here."

And now he was so startled that it set my insides hopping and popping like fat in a fire. I couldn't have said what so filled me with glee. Such glee that it obscured my senses and the neighbour came to perhaps before I did.

"Surely not in that very house?"

"Yes."

"Did you know her?"

"No. No, I didn't. And you?"

He found my question, posed more in levity than suspicion, so uninteresting that he let it pass and asked another one himself:

"But you did know about her, or not?"

"No. I didn't. I chanced on her like you find a mushroom by the wayside. And now I'd like to get hold of a document to certify that she can stay there."

"And what then?"

"I don't know. But why are you asking like this?"

As if having suddenly shed his inhibitions, he looked straight at the woman he'd been talking about. His look spoke greater volumes than his words or his voice and was more gruelling than the words that he couldn't get out. He shook his head and stayed silent.

His rumination was interrupted by the quiet voice of his wife:

"Is it her?"

Oh dear! I'm sure she would rather have whispered it straight in his ear. But it was too late for her to hide it from me. And the mountains and the heavens trembled and also the twilight and my legs and eyes. And it came crashing down on me like the toppling façade of the church.

But now they were ignoring me. Now she was the only one there.

The man was thinking, focussed more on the eyes of his wife than on the woman who had arrived like a lost shadow and was waiting for confirmation that she might stay. But his wife didn't think twice and came straight out with it:

"Is she the Schoolgirl or not?"

Aha!

So not everything had been forgotten. Right. The hair! So she *was* the Schoolgirl. That's what they used to call her. And she'd been top of the class, they said. And that she'd left school with distinction. How could it have been otherwise! And now –

That word! That word! As plain and simple as a pitchfork stuck in your throat! As stark and merciless as the official notice posted on the pillory or over the head of one who's been executed. And now – But now! Surely it was the sweetest and loveliest appellation such as I might never have invented even in my purest dreams! Maybe it is the name that even the angels in Heaven called her. Maybe it is the name by which she would be greeted by the morning dew and the breath proceeding from the mouths of timorous buds as they were aroused from their slumber. At least once I was impelled to whisper it to myself:

"Schoolgirl!"

The local was still shaking his head in confusion. But the moment he heard, or rather just saw the lovely name on my lips, all a-tremble with uncustomary bliss as they were, he jumped up, grabbed me, shook me and shouted into my face:

"Is it really her?"

Nothing. I just smiled. But what at? And why? Oh, my heart! Oh, my confused brain! What to do about you? Nothing now.

Without waiting for an answer he seized my hand in his mighty grip. Well, I withstood the pain, but it did feel as if in my folly I had poked my hand inside a gin trap. It had sprung and now I was caught like a fox. Should I gnaw it off?

But if it were only the hand! Even with the rest of the arm attached! To hell with it! What's a hand? No matter how long a game of blind man's buff it might have taken, I *would* have finally broken out of the magic circle inside which I was spinning, and so perhaps – suddenly, in the nick of time, if not with honour, let alone any appetite – I might have escaped the peril of which I was so afraid. And now the neighbour, with his sudden and unwarranted handshake and the way he was looking into my face, was propelling me towards the gaping throat of a deep pool into which I was meant to jump and was afraid to jump, and would have liked to jump though not knowing whether I should or shouldn't, and the most insidious thing of all was the fact that now I couldn't have offered the slightest resistance. For they just couldn't wait. Especially the women. Even the rose shed some of her diffidence. She approached on tip-toe. She held on to her mother and stood there and blushed, watching me and the woman who had declined to wipe the smudges from my face. And the one with the squirrels? My, how she swung down off the hay cart! She almost seemed to be about to hop up on my shoulder. And those eyes! Those eyes!

I was genuinely trapped. Surely this had to be more than just thanks for some fellow human being's having come to bury the dead. Nor could it be an expression of joy at the return of one for whom they should have been praying and who had now come all this way to see them. It must also have become the celebration of an engagement, which seemed to them definite and inevitable. But who'd given them the idea? Or what was it that had drugged or possessed them? Was it not just a sneaky trick played by the dark beings cavorting around me in an enchanted circle?

Aha, it dawned! Those two wanted to be brides-maids. The horses would have provided our transport. The entire region would have been watching us with all its trackways, river bends and out-of-the-way places, and the lifeless windows would light up for the first time. And there would be bells ringing –

Then I fell into delirium and looked only at her, wanting to see only her. I'm sure my face afforded not a hint of better judgement. My sole impression was that she wasn't in the least surprised and was just waiting to see what I would do next. She may even have been sorry for me, since next her look became mocking, disdainful and inordinately beautiful.

It might have been just a game. Mere delusions of old age. But what a toll it was taking! I myself remained stock still, any movement being that of the glow of evening as it silently died away underfoot, and of the clouds overhead, full of blood and darkness, and yet my being was shot through by the fallen veils of dreams glinting among the shrouds of years and the opal lustre of clay at the bottom of a freshly dug grave, and the clouds kept pausing like thickening smoke bestridden by the night, and the stars kept bursting into song, welcoming the joy that slowly opened its sleepy eyes, and the soul looked on with mute lamentation.

I didn't want to think of anything. Just to dream and stand there like an aged eagle owl as the game was played out. But everything must come to an end. They had already offered us their congratulations. I understood only some of the words and I didn't even thank them. My mind was all confused. And now they took their leave and shook our hands.

So then we went. But why did we keep looking back? What painful yearning, what burning nostalgia, what hope was it that slowed our pace and turned our heads in the direction in which the people had gone? They too kept looking back. They were travelling in the opposite direction, unhurriedly, getting smaller and smaller until they disappeared in the woods. Then darkness fell and I suddenly remembered the name and whispered it to myself:

"Schoolgirl –"

She heard it and glanced at me.

"I'm feeling quite peculiar."

My hair stood on end and I felt as if I'd been walking barefoot and tripped over a shard of something.

"What about?"

"I shouldn't have come back."

"Why not?"

"I shouldn't have told you. I knew I shouldn't be telling you and yet I did. I couldn't help myself. Yesterday, the minute I arrived and saw you, I knew that nothing on earth would stop me from spitting it all out at you."

"Is that all?"

She stopped and looked me straight in the eye.

"Don't make fun of me! You know what I am."

"Yes. Which is why I'm here with you. And as for *how* I make fun of you, you saw that in the graveyard."

Then she touched my hand and placed her fingers in my palm.

"What will happen after you've gone?"

"Why? Where would I go?"

"So please tell me, why you would want to stay?"

"Because I've been snakebitten by you."

I couldn't see into her eyes, but I could detect her beautiful, pensive and agonising smile from her plaintive words:

"That'll pass."

"Well, if it does, you can bite me again."

I uttered this neither in jest, nor in earnest. I'd given it no thought at all. I just happened to be there when it came flying out, bouncing about and dropping down like a dynamited rock. And then, as if it were meant as a final warning, arriving too late, and so the more distressing for it, she said calmly and gravely:

"Just stop making fun of me! You're raising me up to the top of a spire, but you won't be able to hold on to me there. Then you'll have to let me fall."

"Oh, no. If anyone's to fall, it has to be me alone."

Then it came to me, too, in all its fathomless horror. A mute, sullen tower, and arms and legs, and bats circling, waiting for whoever was to fall. And I seemed to be falling alongside her, but I gritted my teeth and gripped her hand. And we spoke no more.

The evening air did speak. It took us compassionately in its embrace and bore us along, along. And the darkness spoke. And the trees looked round and the stream sang to us, something adorably sly and oddly melancholic. The moon came up. It was cold and implacable, but quiet and beautiful like the muteness of death. And the shadows spoke. Our shadows. We were both startled by them, but we couldn't stop looking at them, for they were our shadows, our very own shadows, and it came as a surprise that they could go along together and snuggle up to each other with such calm abandon as if they knew far better than we where we were going, what we desired and what lay ahead. Mine was a little behind like an echo dying out with the despondency of old age, whereas hers bore itself like the triumphant voice of an eternal love song and hope for the future. And should we have been able to pause and let the shadows go on without us, whither they would, they might well have gone on without even looking back, so happy they were, so very happy!

But they were only shadows and apart from them we were there too. We were returning home, if that isn't an overstatement, given that in reality only she was going home. And I?

The closer we came, the less assured were my steps, and the more clearly I discerned the dark majesty of my peril. Oh, how different it all was now, all so different from the evening before, when I was being led by my eyes alone, my overbearing, foolish eyes and my unbridled heedlessness! Now I walked on, not walked, more stumbled, crawled and limped and tottered, but I had to keep going.

Waiting in the house was darkness and door handles and stairs and an impatient silence, irritated to distraction by the nocturnal tunnellings of woodworm and the ticking of the clock. What did the darkness want? What did the door handles and stairs want? What did the silence want?

But I had to keep going.

We were sitting in the kitchen, contemplating the bread and the candle and listening to the persistent ticking of the clock and to the silence of the night. The expression on her face grew ever more pensive and more beautiful and yet I felt death pass close at hand.

Suddenly the clock started and she glanced my way and said:

"Come to bed. We have to be up early."

I shook my head.

"I can't. I wouldn't sleep. You go. Take the candle with you. I don't need it for just me. I prefer wandering about in the dark. I can see better than an eagle owl."

"And what's troubling you?"

"That's my business."

"Couldn't you think of something more cheerful?"

"Gladly! Do you remember what I wanted to do this morning?"

"No. What?"

"Is your memory really that bad?"

"Oh, I know! You kissed me. But only my hand. Then you got scared and ran away. You ran away from me and jumped into the stream. But then to make up you had to stand before me as before God at the Last Judgement."

I don't know if my face flushed, or just my heart. But she had spoken with such sweet, sincere mischievousness that my eyes popped.

"If only I could stand like that before God at the Last Judgement as well – but wait! You'd also have to be there, like this morning."

"I see! And haul you along for good measure."

"Yes. That too. If I were lying right now in my grave and if the trumpet sounded the Last Judgement, I know now that I wouldn't rise, but play deaf and dumb and wait until you came."

"That would take a while. You know what bad time-keepers women are."

"So, I'd just have to wait. Without you I wouldn't dare poke even my nose out."

"What good to you would I be anyway?"

"You might be."

"I don't think I would. You'll be going shirtless."

"But I'd rather go with you."

"Oh, really?"

"Do you remember that apple?"

"Did it taste good?"

"I don't know. At the time I was feeling like a rabid dog."

"Why?"

"I was thinking of you."

"And did it pass?"

"But you saw how it ended up at the cemetery. With me almost devouring your shoes. Weren't you scared."

"I don't know. I may have been. But please don't talk about it."

"Of course. I should be ashamed of myself."

"Why so?"

"It's laughable."

"So I didn't guess wrong."

"What about?"

"That it would pass."

"Pass, not pass. Would you like it to?"

"I don't know what I'd like. But it's better for me to hear it today rather than tomorrow."

"What though?"

"It doesn't seem that laughable to me. I've no idea how it strikes you. But if I were to see or hear right now that you're ashamed of what you did at the cemetery, I'd get up and go this very night and I would walk on and on and never look back."

"Really? You'd leave?"

"Yes. I wouldn't stay here."

"Why not?"

"You need to ask? Everything would remind of the top of that spire with me flapping round it like a filthy rag and scaring the crows."

"Oh dear! You really haven't understood me? Have you no eyes to see? I have so longed for you and looked for you, waited for you and prayed for you. For such a long time now! So very long! Since even before you were born. And when I reached this place, it reached out to touch me from every nook and cranny. But I was so faint that I fell and dropped off and slept as in the grave. But it didn't last long. Because you turned up right then. Your arrival was announced by the hens' clucking and the goat's bleating. Then the stairs began to creak. And the door! That door! And that candle! And you! And then I was all a-tremble –"

"But you were so calm, lying there –"

"Well, I was afraid. It came as quite a shock. And what was I supposed to do? Leap up and grab you? I'm sure it would have been possible. I know that now. Oh, why didn't I do it? It's too late now."

"How so?"

"You've become untouchable to me."

"Of course. You've come to your senses."

"What makes you say that?"

"You know now that I'm a mangy sheep."

"Thank you very much! You'd like to be a mangy sheep, and if I've come to my senses, as you wrongly accuse me of, I have to understand that too. After all, without the mange, there wouldn't be that which makes you so beautiful."

"And what use is it to me?"

"Seriously now. What would you say to a rose, say, if it asked you what use it was to it to be a rose?"

"Nothing. I would remember how, this morning, you first caught a rose's falling petals and how I envied it. And then you dropped them absentmindedly, and I was no longer envious. But would you like to know what I envy now?"

"Of course I would!"

"Only the thing that was in that coffin."

"And what do you envy it for?"

"For the way you held it. Especially the baby. Do you know I was expecting you to bring them back from the dead?"

"No. It's better off where it is."

"Oh, if only you could bury me like that as well!"

"I couldn't."

"Why?"

"No. I couldn't let you go now. Not even in death. Heavens no!"

"And what would you do when I began to putrefy?"

"Well, in that case I'd brick myself in with you so that I couldn't get out even in the unlikely event I might want to."

"But why, for goodness' sake?"

"That needn't concern you. You're not exactly dying yet anyway. I still want you to take me with you several times and show me."

"Show you what?"

"Everything! Everything! I want to see where you were standing when they showed you that document. And the path they took you down. The spot where you crossed yourself. And where you stopped in your tracks having spotted the school. I have to see the recess that was meant to serve as your marriage bed. And the window too. The walls, corners and ceiling, the knots in the floorboards, the scratches and cracks in the door and the holes left in the wall by the ripped-out and mangled hook nails and everything else that drew your weary eyes to it as tears threatened to get the better of them."

"But –"

"I have to know the place. So well as to be able to get there blindfold. I want to go there in the night as well, and if I am to die, I don't want to die anywhere else."

"Do you realise you're scaring me?"

"But I wouldn't be in your way."

"And what would you do?"

"Kneel. Look for you. Imagine your desperate sense of shame. I'd stare at the plaster on the walls, into all the nooks and crannies and at the door handle, and I'd look surreptitiously at the splintered window. I would fall face down with fatigue and kiss the spot where you had lain."

"No. I wouldn't let you."

"Oh, how can you know what a rabid dog feels like! But please, will you also take me to the spot where they killed your mother and where they eventually raped you?"

"Stop! I can't take any more –"

"One more little thing. Don't be afraid! I'd like to see the house where you were forced into service."

"You're tormenting me! Can't you see? You're worse than the devil. What have I done to you?"

"Nothing. I want my portion. And do you know what I'm seeing? You raised high on your triumphal arch, looking out to a point that my trudging feet can never reach. But I won't be fobbed off."

"I can't imagine what you're seeing. I'm just sitting here on this bench and looking only at you."

"And I into you. You are a queen, ignorant of her own true glory."

"And what do I get out of it?"

"For now just hell. Except I'm here now and I want my portion. I'd let you keep the glory. It befits you and you alone. It certainly wouldn't suit me at all, and when it comes to it, I couldn't even bear it on your behalf. So I want the other thing. You can't endure both. I know how it weighs down on you. And I would truly like to bear it for you."

"But what exactly? What? The shame and the mange?"

"Yes. I want to swallow it and burn in it, drown in it, or wear it on my face like a plague bubo."

"But this is blasphemy! Doesn't it strike you that you're rambling?"

"All I want from you is that which oppresses and pains you. Where's the sin in that?"

"And aren't you afraid?"

"And suppose my lips rotted away and my nose dropped off! Do you want me to swear how glad I would be to endure that? I'd merely be bearing that which you bear in your heart and eyes. Those eyes that still only look back in search of your mother."

"But how do you imagine it?"

"That depends on you."

"Only on me? Oh, no! If I weren't fit and well, I'd understand it and swallow it. If I were so blind that I'd –"

"Please, don't say it! I so longed for you and looked for you, waited for you and prayed for you even back then when you'd never even been heard of. Before you were born. Ever since your childhood. Oh, if only I'd known I would find you here! But what was I meant to do? No star led me to this spot, and if I ever came close enough just to let out a shout and trip down from the hilltops, any response from this direction came in a hard, alien language and a look of disapproval. But you grew up here to blossom forth, and after you'd breathed your fill of the sweet air, the clouds and stars and begun to observe uneasily your own virginal beauty, came a day and came a night and they killed your mother and trampled on your face. Well, that had been ordained from the first day when you looked down from God's rainbow into my boyhood dreams. It had to be. Yes, had to. Without it we probably wouldn't have met. And if perchance we had met, we wouldn't have recognised each other."

"And how did you recognise me?"

"Do you know what I wanted here?"

"Well, if memory serves, it was to regret certain sins –"

"But only those not committed. Or rather the fact that, despite all the weeping and whining of the senses and despite all the attempted begging, I have yet to be admitted to the place where there is fire and flame and where, whether with ostentation or just modestly, I might flare up however briefly like burning turnip tops. That is what propelled me all the way here so that in peace and isolation I might contemplate whether I really am so old that I can now digest only diluted grace or whether I may hope for the miracle of finally succeeding in committing such a great sin that it would cry to high heaven."

"And that would be a miracle?"

"And how! I am old and today I only fancy such sins as will shine out in eternity as a token of honour. However, they are so rare that they haven't yet been accomplished to my liking, nor will they be even at the hour of death. What to do about it? Hm, what indeed! The ashes are still hot and the heart is writhing. So why should it not try to exact that which it seeks so desperately? That single sin! That miracle of all sins!

"And that would be a sin?"

"By now, certainly. As recently as yesterday it might have still been a game for me. Wanting was enough. But I didn't want! And the candle showed me what I ought to do and how. And I didn't do it! I'd only have lost that which I don't have a clue what to do about: my heart. And now I could be looking at you and laughing and might never find out what you really are."

"And has it passed now?"

"Oh, do stop making fun of me! You've got eyes. You're a woman. You must have seen at the cemetery the way I kissed your breath and stroked your voice. But why go into that now! That's enough!"

"And that sin?"

"Thanks for reminding me. I might almost have thought that a sin like that was just a delusion of an unhinged mind. That it was just an illusion, that it had no real substance, that it merely beckoned from a distance like Heaven's rainbow, encircling the world but itself untouchable. And lo and behold! I've got it now. I don't know how I've come this far, and why it should be me. And I can't claim that it's something I've dreamed of. You're alive. I can see you. You have scrubbed my back and tucked me under a duvet. I have stolen the apple you'd already bitten into, I've kissed your shoes, clasped your heels and now here we are, sitting together and eating and chatting. But if I wanted to do now what I missed out on yesterday, it would be the most amazing sin, such as has never been and never will be committed."

"Aha! Not that miracle, by any chance?"

"The very one."

"I'm surprised."

"The point being that I know now that for me you are sacrosanct. I want only to be your servant and squat in a corner."

"And nothing else?"

"It's sufficient to my needs."

"Hm!"

"Don't go thinking I won't be on fire. My fire will never go out till the day I die. And I wouldn't want it to. But I'll curl up like that viper yesterday and I might, if you tread on my head once in a while, thrash about and unravel, but I'll certainly do you no harm. I desire no other joy than that you'll keep me here."

"And why are you so modest?"

"And what more could I want?"

"That miracle."

"No."

"Are you scared of it?"

"Now I see you somewhere else. Now you glory in all the adornment of the beatified, as on a marble column and in golden armour. Surely there could be no more cruel and evil temptation than the idea of clambering up, grabbing you and falling down with you. But what's the use! I see that I am only a scorpion."

"And if it were so, so what? Do wake up! You will see that the column is of clay and the armour rusted through with my shame and mange."

"*You* wake up! You are a queen, ignorant of your true glory –"

"And what use is that to me! I am troubled."

"Suffer away! It's something you have to put up with."

"Thank you very much! I'd happily go without. But what's stopping you?"

"You're high up, so very high –"

"Knock me down then!"

"Oh, no! Anyone could do that. The really wretched thing is that the sin that would blow a hole in the heavens can't be committed in a random state of ecstasy or when the spirit is giddy, but only in the manner in which insects do it."

"And isn't that precisely where the miracle lies?"

"Be that so or be it not, I certainly wouldn't concern myself as to whether it's a sin once I'd climbed up that column and snatched you towards me. And why should I fear for my wretched soul anyway? After all this is you! And if I am to fall, why shouldn't I fall for your sake? That's surely not such a wicked thing. But that's not how I imagine it. I know what suits each of us. You light, me shade. You golden armour, me shame and mange. After all, I'm old, and if it were to come to pass that I should in my derangement perform a miracle and commit that sin, then the devil must surely be amazed and make fun of me, and all those consorts might then come and spit in my face –"

"And you wouldn't want that –"

She'd said it. As I'd anticipated: she'd been looking at me with such tenderness and derision, sweetness and disdain that I couldn't have expected anything other than that she would snake-bite me. This was a turn for the worse. My heart was as twisted as a dish-rag. But it wasn't giving in yet.

"Oh, but I would. But differently. Not on your account, but on mine."

"I get it now. You are noble, magnanimous and you certainly also have some authority and you want to play games. With me, too. Why not? But you see, well –"

She stopped short. Perhaps her malice had worn her down and left her short of breath.

I stood up. I was trembling. I felt as if I were challenging death and all around me I could sense the eyes of invisible beings observing me, me alone. And how! And at the same time I was being observed by *her* eyes, full of surprise, distrust and unbounded malignity, and by the flame of that candle.

And I was suffocating on my own defiance. By now I was peering into the abyss and sensing that I could not and must not retreat, I asked:

"How many of them were there?"

She may not have understood immediately.

"How –"

"You don't know?"

I watched as she reddened.

"Erm, lots."

"So many that in the time that has elapsed you've even forgotten roughly how many?"

"Oh, no, that's not something that's forgotten lightly! I know exactly how many."

"So, how many?"

"No! Don't ask!"

"So just tell me yourself."

"Surely this is something that not even the lewdest whore would let on about. Least of all to you."

"And you?"

"Are you the devil?"

"And if I were?"

"Enough! Please, stop!"

"What are you afraid of? Can you really want to hold on to those memories till your dying day as a memento? Despite all the heartache, are they still somehow dear to you? Go on, say it! Don't be afraid of me! I don't have anyone else. Only you."

She tossed her head.

"Are you sure you're not a priest?"

"No, I'm not. And if I were, I wouldn't let it bother you."

"I'd tell you of my own accord."

"And I'd tell you I hadn't asked."

"And I *would* tell you! I would! I would!"

"But it wouldn't be confession."

"What then?"

"Surely you know that better than I. Anyway, I am *not* a priest and you're *not* in the confessional here."

"But it's not something you'd say outside the confessional."

"You don't have to say anything. Just hold on. I'll do the counting."

"But what are you going to do? You're not going to beat me, are you?"

"Beat? Goodness, no! Kiss, yes, only kiss you! And keep kissing you until you say 'Stop!'"

The moon approached the window and peeked inside. And I beheld countless spectres approaching as out of a plague-engendered fog. Then they, having prepared this astounding moment for us, stood about us, their toady eyes fixed on my puffy lips, and waited for me to lay her on her back and kneel down to embrace her as a leper's corpse.

But suddenly I saw the light.

No. She wasn't watching me. By this stage she'd covered her eyes. And within me something jerked, barked and squeaked and my teeth chattered, for I'd seen the Book of Life lying open and I sensed about me the eyes of invisible beings living and dead, and at that moment she alone, alone she would not have glanced at my hideous features, not for anything in the world.

Of course I wasn't going to give up. But then she said, with such disdain that my blood flared up in a jagged flame:

"And what would be the point, for either of us? What do you suppose it would be? It's something that's only done for love, or more as a bit of naughty fun. Yet you want to make a virtue of it?"

But now I was sitting down, holding on to the table so as not to collapse into nothingness, and with some effort I stammered:

"No, no, not a virtue! That's not what I want."

"What then? You must know that this isn't going to help me. Let alone you. It isn't something superficial. It's in the heart and soul. But what can I hope for?"

"Everything," I said, scoffing at my own desperate wretchedness. "Fear not. Your time will come. But don't be too particular! You are *so* beautiful – and I am old now!"

"You're telling me that?"

"Yes."

"You?"

"Yes."

"Well, thank you. I don't really know who I am, but you seem to want to make me into a whore."

"What *can* you be thinking? Do you know what that would make me? Just a disgusting old man who has yielded to his own ardour and is now drowning in something that is no longer passion, but the desperation of the dying."

"And you wouldn't want that –"

Hm, that stung. It sank all the way into my lung tissue. But still I didn't yield.

"Please don't go thinking that I'd give you up afterwards! Afterwards never! Never ever! But thereafter I'd never be more than a monstrous fomenter of your sleepless hours and the darkness of your days."

"And you believe that?"

"Oh, do stop making fun of me! If I knew I were to die! If I knew I were to die if not today, then at least this year. But suppose I were to hang around for a number of years?"

"And would that bother you?"

"It's not up to me! My spirit is weary and my conscience would doubtless be entirely willing to adjust. Why not? It's not unheard-of. But of course you'd only be liberated by my death. But when?"

"And you'd like to die?"

"That's the most pathetic thing about it! Afterwards I probably wouldn't want to. But suppose I did! You know from experience that life is tough and death doesn't come at our bidding."

"And is that so bad? After all, I'd be hanging around here with you."

"But there's one thing you're forgetting. I'm not one of yours. I'm alien. So alien –"

"Ah, don't say that!"

"Why not?"

"Didn't they sell me off?"

"Haven't you forgiven them yet?"

"That's not the point! Long ago. Given that it was nothing they wouldn't have done to their own children. But it's not something that's easily forgotten. And even if I did forget, it's too late now."

"No. You must realise that blood calls to blood only with the voice of its ancestors. It doesn't respond to a voice that's alien. Before an alien voice even bones grow cold, before such a voice the dust on one's shoes grows cold, before such a voice even one's shadow grows cold."

"What *are* you talking about?"

"I learned this today at first hand. How defiantly did your bones and joints show me that they're different from the ones that I see back in my own part of the world! Even those stockings were suggestive of a different air, a different region, a different Heaven and Hell. And those shoes! They seemed to be telling me: Go! What do you want here? You're an alien! And the dust! How it resisted my lips and my tears! No, no! Not you! You'd be alien even in Heaven. And that so irked me that I'd rather have suffocated than let go of you."

"So now you see!"

"I do. I see how old I am. How weak I am. And also so very alien! It's you who can't see. Do you know what it would lead to?"

"Better than you do, I'm sure. I've had quite enough of those who are young and strong, and I don't want to hear about our people till the day I die."

"You're wrong. You don't surprise me though. I'm also only human. But we can't change things. I'm sure I'd only disgust you. After all, I do know myself."

"Can I ask you something?"

"Why not?"

"Have you had any children?"

Taken aback, I shifted my position. How like a woman!

"Yes."

"How many?"

"Only five."

"Five children! And haven't you understood that a child is everything? Dear me, can a man, no matter how bad he might be, be disgusting to the mother of his children?"

"I don't know."

"So let me tell you, but don't hold it against me afterwards! The man who was the father of my child – did I tell you I had one? He was older than you. Certainly older than you. He was already toothless, hard of hearing, his head shook and he dribbled. But believe me, I never once found it funny. No. Never. I even had to get up with him and see him out of the door so he didn't trip over something.

The clock clacked. Perhaps it was death tripping up. But it passed her by. She still hadn't said her all.

"Anyway, I was scared they might just dump me somewhere, baby and all."

Suddenly, from above us, came such a joyous cuckooing as if the child had peeped out from the tranquillity of its resting place and let out a shriek, having recognised its mother's voice. Then it happily went on to cuckoo out to us the sum of hours lost, the sum of years lost and love lost. And it might have been laughing so hard, or it might have been sobbing so hard, that its voice quavered and with it the darkened corners and the beams and the ceiling also began to quaver.

"So you see," she went on, her voice as sweet as if she were already standing at the gates of Paradise, "your head doesn't shake and you don't dribble. You're a fine gentleman. But what do you actually want? My shame? What will you do with it?"

As she spoke, it was like a bear's paws stroking me, running lovingly not now over my bare skin, but over my brain, my entrails and my naked arteries, and I felt about to faint and fall as beneath the gallows.

But she wasn't letting me go yet.

"You *were* wrong, weren't you? Don't be shy! Admit it! You know what *I* am, and I know what *you* are. But please don't interrupt me. You're a grand gentleman. You're kind and you've taken me for a lost child. And if that were all! You have eyes and you can divine that I too have a heart. Everything could be possible. Why not? You *are* a man. You don't recoil from me. You would happily leap into my shame and bathe in it and come out as clean as the flame of that candle. But who can tell what would come next. *That's* the bad thing. What would be the outcome? Not even I could assure you that there'd be no outcome. I know that you don't recoil from me. I know that in my company you regard yourself as nothing. But a baby! Ah, a baby! Your little baby! Just imagine what it would have to germinate in, what paths its innocent eyes would have to follow before it saw the light of day. What would it press its innocent lips to inside there before they began to breathe! It could even choke to death! It might have to die and decompose instead like the baby in that coffin! So, could you cope with that? No. I see now myself why I can't want it."

Ah, those infernal, venomous and oh-so-sweet eyes! How decorously they shone! How contritely they confessed to their demure distress! How they begged for forgiveness! And those raised eyelids! How cruelly they brought to my mind all the pride and beauty and even the contours of God's rainbow, the very one that had ignited my boyhood yearning, finally setting it ablaze before fading away itself! And that voice! Oh, that voice!

"Just let me keep my shame! Let me keep my manginess! That way I've got something at least. Otherwise I'd have nothing."

How like a woman.

I would gladly have responded, but some invisible and sublime hand covered my mouth. And I wished that she might say something, charging my perverted soul with meanness and giving testimony to the same, and that we might be standing before God in judgement and that she might lay all the blame on me alone, for in her voice there was so much glory and beatitude that I no longer wished to hear anything but that voice.

But now it had subsided. With lips parted and drooping, I clasped my hands and listened to its echo coming from the ends from which eternity itself calls. And suddenly all the heights of dreams and the depths of melancholy began to sing and I heard bells and the murmuring of waters and the vibration of rays passing through the cool veil of death, the footsteps of fragrance and longing, the breath of the rainbow and tears, the lamentation of faded felicity, the sadness of unanswered prayers, and that entreaty. That entreaty! And I saw the Book of Life lying open, with a drafted, but unsigned contract, and souls, or shades, waiting, without daring to speak, to see what *I* would do. Also waiting were the walls and ceiling and the moon and stars. But upon my shoulders I could feel the iniquitous burden of my years, and in my heart the sediment of blood and the ooze of dead scorpions, and that of which those heights of dreams and depths of melancholy were singing suddenly vanished to that place where the only mercy is the embrace of death.

And I called out to the viper as my only confidant and true sibling, but in vain. No, it wasn't there. I looked for the coffin and the maggots and the grave, likewise in vain. So instead I wanted to keep my eyes peeled for the invisible beings who were guarding the open Book of Life, watching my every move.

But suddenly I froze. What's this? It had quite disappeared. They had borne the book away with them without so much as a word of farewell. So now I was alone and no echo of weeping came from any side, nor suppressed laughter, nor any other sign beyond the drillings of woodworm and the rustlings of moths. But where was the marble column? Where the golden armour? Where the glory and the power?

I could scarcely grasp that this was nothing but a warning that from now on no one would give me any sign, nor could they, no matter how I begged and pleaded; that the moment was nigh when I, and I alone, should show whether or not I desired to burn away on a pyre in the abandoned temple of my pride like worthless turnip tops, or whether or not I would accept that from which my wariness was making me flee, even though my desire for it was so powerful that it debilitated my blood.

And yet I wasn't entirely alone! There was the candle. The mysterious, unsullied and hallowed candle that the night before had cast its compassionate light upon me as upon a sleeping bat. That was the start of something that could not end. Now it cast its light in the selfsame manner upon the white-clothed table and the water and the bread. And in the same manner it was lighting up my entire being. It was quiet and beautiful, like the daystar before the break of day, like a last smile, like pain and snow. And then I realised that the candle's flame was admiring itself in my eyes and warming my face like the sweetest breath, and I clasped my hands together.

It was standing in the middle of the table, but I had an unerring sense that, with the totally pure face of its flame that was whispering secret messages of love, it

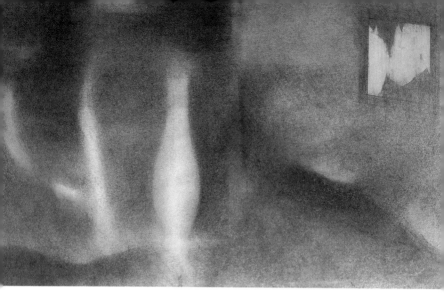

kept turning towards me and seeking out me alone. And I watched it and stroked the table. Then I pulled the candlestick towards me and stroked the candle. It was alive and the noise within it sounded like the enchanted echo of the blissful buzzing of bees. Then I gripped it so hard that it arched, surprised by the perfidy of my fervour. The flame jumped and in its terror cried into the darkness for help. I placed my palm against it from the side, nipped off the burnt stub of its wick and the candle ceased resisting and became endearing, yielding to its wistful trust in mercy. And the flame now radiated all the coyness of a virgin in that lost instant when she doesn't know that this is her last radiance before being violated.

At first it shone but shyly, still flickering. But then with childlike trust it snuggled up to my palm and began to laugh so sweetly and rosily that I was overcome with weeping. And that was unsurprising. How could it have failed to overcome me? For I knew what it wanted. It was the image of a soul that has longed to descend and has been seeking out her who would proffer her crotch. And now it was pleading and begging for her and showing me her innocent face and promising something of which only a flame or a spirit knows how to speak. And then I cupped the flame in both hands and the flame glowed through them as through the glass of a sanctuary lamp. And I would have grasped it had I not feared that it might be snuffed out before the hardest part had begun.

Then the clock made a noise and the hand on the dial sprang for dear life to the menacing line that death had stamped on it as the command either for leave-taking or for instant copulation. And it was as abrupt as a call to start a game when everything is ready and he who is to play is still in a haze. The shadows were chilled with fear, the moon looked aside and the seconds dripped away like blood-imbrued sweat into the cauldron of death.

But the game was beginning. For now, only the flame spoke. It spoke clearly and plainly and I was expected to respond to it. It was already waiting. Easy now! Let not a single flicker of that timidly rising, demure star go to waste, for it cannot be repeated.

Yet what was my response to be? How on earth does one greet a soul who has longed to descend and has been seeking a being that will proffer its crotch! By words alone?

Oh, no! Are words at all up to embracing a flame?

No! I raised the candle to the very edge of my lips. Then I held my breath and kissed the flame. At first timidly and just once, like a faint-hearted, lovesick creature who knows neither where he is nor how he got there, when at the most opportune moment and in the most romantic spot he spots the object of his dreams and sees that she's asleep. And then the candle too seemed to me to be sleeping. It was dreaming of the beauty of the stars, maybe it was saying a secret prayer, and it didn't even hurt.

I'd been kissing naught but my own breath. Then I half-closed my eyes and kissed the candle twice in succession. It smelled like fallen leaves and the breath of withered roses and it jabbed more impatiently than a jealous thorn that also longs to be kissed. My lips swelled with bliss and the sweetness of fire, sparks flew from my eyes and my smile contracted.

This time I was kissing blood. And now my heart started up! Not once, not twice, but three times! Aah!

Now it was smarting like the shame that stings. Oh, my heart! Oh, my soul! Do come now, will you? Just come!

At that moment, though, from beyond the fire there was a sudden cry:

"What are you doing? Are you mad?"

And the fire was torn from the lamp of my cupped hands and their light went out.

"I say," I said reproachfully, "aren't I even allowed to singe my nose now?"

An uncertain smile flitted across her lips, only to vanish at once.

"Don't make fun of me! You could seem to be making fun of something that is dearer than shame."

"Oh come now. I saw the candle even before I saw you. Its radiance was what prepared me for your arrival. So why shouldn't I offer it my thanks? Or are you jealous of it? Why?"

"I don't know. I'm afraid."

"Now there's a thing! Me too. But my fear is more toxic. There are two voices inside me. I don't know which one is lying. One keeps on saying that I'm nothing but a parasite and an unclean louse, and the other tells me that I'm nothing but an oafish, pathetic servant. The truth is probably what the first one says. But I can't be sure and it seems unlikely I'll find out until what is to come does come."

"Wha – ?"

She broke off. That tiny interrogative couldn't make it past her lips, though it was no longer than the click of a clock. But she couldn't salvage it now. What she had *not* said revealed itself by her consternation. What now? Probably nothing. She blanched, lowered her gaze and pressed her lips together. Her hand attempted to slope away off the cloth down under the table to hide in the semi-darkness. But even that failed. And if that were all! The clock clicked and what she hadn't dared utter herself was suddenly broadcast out loud by the cuckoo:

"What's that?"

Oh dear!

I might have risen and walked round the table. I might have knelt down, kissed her and whimpered happily. But for now I wanted to hear the elation alone. Oh, seconds, cut the clamour! You're not the only ones here! Why don't you go to bed?

But the seconds didn't obey me, for they could see for themselves the pressed lips and the lowered gaze, and much better than I. But I wavered no more and said:

"The baby."

She may not have understood me at first. She didn't even blink, merely holding her breath and staring hard at the crumbs on the tablecloth. Then I advanced my hand to the middle of the table and opened it wide.

Again there was silence and paleness and stupefaction, and words that declined to venture to the rim of my lips. But my open palm was getting impatient. It wanted to speak for itself, and it motioned with its forefinger.

When she saw it, she gave a shiver and I had a sense that the shadow of death had passed her by. And I was troubled, but I swallowed my concerns and said:

"So what now?"

Perhaps she really didn't know where she was and what was happening and what I wanted from her. Only slowly did she ease her hand towards my palm, a bit like when a snake isn't certain enough about a possible danger to crawl all the way out. By the time it reached its destination and my palm closed on it, crushing it more inexorably than a poacher's trap, it was too weak even to attempt to tear free and there in the palm of my hand it lay upon my soul and love like a corpse upon a pyre. It was cold and damp like a killed fish. But then it jerked, as in sleep, nestled warily up to the palm and began testing whether it mightn't still be asleep and whether it shouldn't wake up. Then it began to shake, lightly and feverishly at first, then violently and laboriously, until finally the whole table shook and with it my elbows.

My, such shaking! I wondered if I would shake like that when the leaden breath of death cast my soul,

twisted like a frost-damaged leaf, right into the open palm of God. Oh, such shaking! I should be down on my knees thinking of it and giving thanks for it.

There was a holy silence. And I wouldn't have dared look at her, fearful of committing sacrilege. Even the candle flame shrank down and bated its breath. But then, all of a sudden, she banged her head limply on the table and burst into tears.

That made the palm of my hand twitch. But should I have got up? No. I shouldn't. Or say something? What though? Whose tears were they? Mine perhaps? No, no. What if they did soak into the tablecloth! What of it! The rainbow that was meant to emerge from them had already risen and was enfolding us in its embrace. Enfolding and warming us, intoxicating us with its sublime glow, with its mercy that passeth all understanding, and with all its glory like the Beatitudes. And I would have been afraid. I would have fallen down and cried: Get Thee behind me! Lead me not into temptation! I am unclean, duplicitous and evil as a serpent, and it would be intolerable if in return I accepted while still living that which Thou affordest only in paradise. That would surely be a punishment worse than hell. Oh, be not so merciless! Let me die even as a rabid dog, but punish me not with insanity!

But a mysterious hand covered my mouth and I suddenly saw the light. Who was to receive, in exchange for all the heartache and all the humiliation, the reward of beatitude? Surely not I! She alone had a claim upon everything, not excepting my miserable self, my dying breath and all my blood, if only for the extirpation of the terrible injury that she bore within her, or for the new life which was to spring from her body as the most gracious recompense. It probably mattered not in the slightest now what I was. I was what I was. And were an order to have been given that, brooking no delay, I should myself take her down from the marble column, remove the golden armour from her and take her to myself, in vain would I have resisted, for orders are orders and I would have had to act.

I rose, walked round the table and dropped to my knees. She offered no resistance when I thrust my head right into her lap. I half-closed my eyes and I felt good. But she suddenly collected herself, withdrew her hand from the table and, eyes closed and guided by my lineaments and breath, she sought out my eyes and lips. Then gently and chastely she raised me towards her heart. And now I heard an entire cascade of tears and blood and bliss and her apprehension and impatience, though by now I was incapable of distinguishing whose heart was yelling and whose was singing.

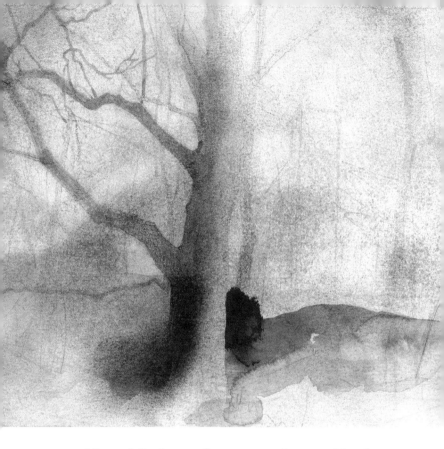

Meanwhile the candle was guttering, our blood was abating and our senses brightening. But I could still feel as a weakening spasm the delicate tremor in the hand with which she was shyly clasping my eager lips to her slackening heart and I had to wait. Once calm descended, I squeezed out from under the clutch of that lovely hand like a regenerated snake, upwards over her breast, and I saw the luminescent and mystical glitter of her red hair and a delicate rose petal on her face. And I took a deep breath and began to stutter:

"But at least two in due course! It would be sad with just the one –"

She flushed, gazed into my imploring eyes and gave a slight, sweet smile. Then she half-closed her eyes and slowly drew my silly head to her beautiful lips. Then she stopped breathing. And suddenly she kissed me. Just once at first, shyly, like a –

Completed on All Saints' Day 1955.

AFTERWORD:

IRA ET IRIS SEU LITTERA GESTA DOCET

In our own times, literature and cinema have become increasingly preoccupied with imagining the responses of human beings in a post-apocalyptic landscape after environmental or nuclear disaster or war. These stories often focus on the chance encounter of a small number of survivors, whose actions may ultimately offer a tentative hope that human society can be rebuilt, perhaps in a less harmful or self-destructive way. After 1945, fractured and devastated post-war Europe provided this context for real. For some, the answers lay in more 'progress', more 'modernity': new social and economic orders, greater international cooperation and the development of human rights law. For the author of *God's Rainbow*, however, the path to recovery and renewal lay not in new models, but in what twentieth-century Europe had, in his view, forgotten, abandoned or distorted: the God who set his bow in the sky as a sign of his love, mercy and forgiveness, to seal his covenant with Noah after the Flood that he would never again destroy the world. In *God's Rainbow*, the wanderer-narrator enters a postdiluvian landscape, a site of death, destruction and decay that – through repentance, atonement and reconciliation – becomes a place of renewal, redemption and rebirth.

A particular challenge to the contemporary reader is that everything in the novel appears in this Baroque-influenced, dual perspective of death and rebirth, terrestrial and celestial, evil and good. In the first, most difficult chapter, the reader accompanies the narrator as he is taken away from the mundane, one-dimensional material world into a space where everything appears in both a real and symbolic guise, where both must learn to see things differently. The narrator, unsure what has prompted his journey or what its purpose might be, is simultaneously a hiker and a Dantean pilgrim, led by the stirring of his soul into 'the borderlands of hell', an undulating desert where he expects to be tempted, but which will become the site of his salvation. The serpent guarding the threshold, however, recalls not only the Devil in the Garden of Eden, but also the wisdom that will replace the 'better judgement' the narrator has lost, and – for Jaroslav Durych, a physician by profession – healing. The narrator will eventually find the purpose of his journey in an apparently abandoned house by a stream, a symbol of life and hope, but also of the crossing into the underworld, where he is woken in the night by a light that signals the arrival of a young woman whose 'hellish' red hair signifies temptation, even witchcraft, but also initiation into mystical knowledge.

In the decades following the novel's first publication in 1969, the dominant critical interpretation sought to cut through its deliberately complex imagery, symbolism and patterns of thought and emphasise its implicit historical context: the initially violent, unregulated deportation of over two million Bohemian Germans from Czechoslovakia in 1945. Durych names neither the setting nor its characters, nor reveals their ethnicity, but the action of the novel takes place in identifiable places in the northern Bohemian borderlands or Sudetenland, where the majority of Czechoslovakia's Bohemian Germans lived until the end of the Second World War. Durych came to the Lusatian Mountains, about one hundred kilometres north of Prague, close to the border with Germany and Poland, in July 1947 and for a very low price bought a cottage in Dolní Světlá (Nieder Lichtenwalde) previously owned by German weavers, where he would spend most of the warmer half of each year until his death in 1962. His decision to leave Prague for rural solitude resembles his narrator's departure in the novel, and might even be understood as an actualization of the 'internal exile' into which he was effectively sent after 1945. In his letters, however, Durych accepts the opportunity to withdraw (at a time when other intellectuals associated with Roman Catholicism and conservative nationalism faced imprisonment and hard labour), and presents the ascetic simplicity of his solitude almost as a form of religious retreat.

The significance of the setting is intensified by similarities between the narrator and author: both are widowers over sixty years old with five children and were supposed to have become priests. From the outset, Durych did not expect that the book would be published in his lifetime; indeed, he hid the manuscript under a pile of coal in the cellar of his house in Prague for fear that its contents would cause him problems. The private nature of the book perhaps explains why, unlike in most of his previous fiction, he uses a first-person narration and so many allusions to crucial, intimate aspects of his own life. In particular, the rainbow light of a fairytale world, first encountered in his *Memories of Youth* (1928), is linked for the author with the early death of his mother, whom he knew only from vague memories, dreams and the accounts of others. In the first draft of *God's Rainbow*, the narrator tells the young woman that while she fears the moon, because of the trauma she experienced at night, he fears the afternoon sun, which reminds him of his mother's funeral.

The description of the narrator's journey in the novel corresponds very precisely to the local reality. The narrator comes from the nearest town; this is Cvikov (Zwickau in Böhmen), where Durych used to go to confession to the local parish priest, Josef Dobiáš, with whom he formed a close relationship and to whom he even confided his plans to write the book. In a letter to Durych dated December 27th 1955, Dobiáš writes:

I think of you most of all and very vividly in Mařenice in connection with *God's Rainbow*. The area, now covered in snow, looks very sad compared to the summer, but the attendance in church at Christmas was surprisingly large this year, apparently the largest for many years. Perhaps souls are softening and the rainbow of God, of reconciliation and forgiveness, will also appear here.

It is in Mařenice (Groß-Mergthal) that the narrator finds the coffin with the unburied, decomposing body. The description of the church with one tower corresponds precisely to the Church of Mary Magdalene, a name which undoubtedly resonated with Durych's preoccupations in the novel. Other locations are not so unequivocally identifiable, but the description of the school, the proximity of the border and the walk taken through the village by the two protagonists suggest Krompach (Krombach), a village neighbouring Dolní Světlá and Mařenice.

The precise setting lends authenticity to the story told by the young woman. She suspects the narrator of wanting to steal from her or drive her out, a realistic enough allusion to the Czech 'gold-diggers' who travelled to North Bohemia after the liberation. She also gives further indications of her ethnicity, protesting: 'I was born right here, alongside you [...] can't you tell by my accent?' She retells her fate only in possessive pronouns, but we can deduce that 'our people' – logically the defeated Germans – handed her over to 'them'

– presumably liberating Soviet soldiers – who held her for a week in her school, where she was repeatedly raped. She was then taken home by 'your [the narrator's] lot' – the Czechs – who killed her mother as she tried to escape, then raped her while she stared into her dying mother's eyes before killing her mentally handicapped aunt.

These emblematic details about the actions of both the Red Army and Czechs in the Sudetenland at the end of the war were not discussed in Czechoslovakia at the time of writing, and indeed have only come substantially to light since the fall of Communism; in this respect, Durych's novel is ground-breaking. Historians have not been able to link the woman's story to a single, real-life case, though in the first draft of the novel Durych includes many details left out of the final version. Given that information about a similar, lengthy collective rape can be found in certain accounts about the liberation given by expelled Bohemian Germans, Durych may have drawn on a real-life episode that shocked even a writer who, as a military doctor, had experienced the Eastern Front in the First World War and written in depth about the horrors of the Thirty Years War, in a historical novel translated into English in 1935 as *The Descent of the Idol*. It is possible that the woman's story is composed from the fates of several German women; a local eye-witness account from Krompach reports that in 1945, during the liberation, a Soviet soldier raped the daughter of a German family and, when her father intervened, shot her mother to frighten him off.

Neither the publisher's internal reader reports on the manuscript from the 1960s nor post-publication reviews of the novel in 1969 and 1970 make reference to the implicit historical context. Perhaps it was not obvious to readers who believed, like the narrator of *God's Rainbow*, that the whole matter had been satisfactorily resolved, but more likely it was too politically sensitive to mention. In 1975, however, the dissident thinker, Jan Patočka, oversaw the publication of the novel in German translation in an ostensibly unsuccessful attempt amid the Cold War to overcome entrenched national positions and initiate a Czech-German dialogue that might lead to the reconciliation promised by the text. The German translation provided something of an artistic alibi for the German side at a time when thousands of Czechs who did not want to live under Soviet-led occupation after 1968 followed the expelled Bohemian Germans into West German exile. Patočka's afterword, which makes the historical context of the novel explicit, has accompanied every subsequent Czech edition and the French translation too.

Though important for broader cultural-political reasons, *God's Rainbow* is more than a documentary testament about the Czech role in atrocities relating to the Second World War and its subsequent moral condemnation, and the literal, historical reading does not do full justice to how Durych, an experienced writer still at the peak of his powers aged 69, combines the historical, ethical, allegorical and mystical to overcome this apparently unending, destructive cycle of blame. In June 1945, at the village of Lidice, on the third anniversary of the worst German atrocity against the occupied Czechs, at the very time that violence against Bohemian Germans of the type described by the young woman was taking place, the Czechoslovak president, Edvard Beneš, justified the expulsion of all Bohemian Germans from Czechoslovakia on the grounds of their 'collective guilt', their shared responsibility for an 'indelible, unforgivable sin'. In *God's Rainbow*, Durych seeks to correct this distortion of Christian language and concepts. In 1939, he had written:

> Everything that is good about democracy, progress, humanism and universal ideals has from first to last been stolen from Christian teaching; if they had not robbed Christian teaching, they would have nothing to show off about and herein lies the worst shamelessness, that those who want to destroy Christianity had first to rob it and then present what they had stolen as their own superiority.

In a novel written as this attempted destruction of Christianity was reaching its peak in Stalinist Czechoslovakia, Durych reasserts that guilt, repentance and atonement are not merely discrete, empty rhetorical phrases, but essential components of an approach to life that endlessly enables the human being to heal, be healed and begin again in his relationships with others and with God, a way of being that the so-called civilised world has, in his view, fatally abandoned.

A study of the six surviving drafts of the novel, held in the archive of the Museum of National Literature (Památ-ník národního písemnictví) in Prague, reveals how Durych gradually erases the traces of a story set in a real time and place and moves it to the level of a fairy-tale timelessness, thereby rendering the action allegorical, transferable to any traumatic context. The mystical is suggested by allusions not only to the Scriptures – the two protagonists as Adam and Eve – but also to the Roman Catholic liturgy. The quotations from the Dies irae at the beginning of the novel evoke the atmosphere of a funeral. The Lord's Prayer and Salve Regi-na mark the culmination of the melancholy confession and burial scene. The narrator is slow to grasp his connection to the young woman's horrific experiences and to recognize the sin of 'his people' as his own. Then, apparently to chas-tise himself, he presses her against her will to reveal every detail, but in keeping with the all-pervading ambivalence in the novel, Durych suggests that what torments may also heal. The woman refers to the narrator sarcastically as her 'confessor', but by speaking of what happened to her, she too is freed from suffering. Though her confession may remind contemporary readers more of Jungian 'talking therapy' and the 'search for closure', such notions would, for Durych, exemplify what he considers the pale imitation of Christian models in godless modernity. She joins the narrator in his punishing act of penance, and they bury the coffin, the embodiment of all the wrongs left unrepented in this place, together. Rid of these burdens, the protagonists can overcome the seemingly insurmountable differences between them and build a fruitful relationship founded in shared humanity. Only once they have been absolved do the first man and woman of this newly recovered Eden encounter other people, who must have been present before, but only now become partners in the communal life of this newly settled land. When they first meet, the reader senses hostility, but once it becomes clear that the 'hermit' knows who the 'schoolgirl' is and accepts her as such, relations between all the people present are restored. God's rainbow (*iris* in Latin), which follows the cataclysm of God's rage (in Latin, *ira*) is set in the sky over the human beings once again charged with tending God's earth.

In the Christian tradition, reading teaches action (*littera gesta docet*). In *God's Rainbow*, Durych, who between the wars had been one of the most penetrating, but also at times unforgiving and aggressive critics of the First Czechoslovak Republic petty-bourgeois establishment, tries with humility to show how even the most tragic wrongs in human history can always be overcome if human beings rediscover their place in the Absolute. In writing *God's Rainbow*, Durych became one of very few Czech post-war intellectuals who, despite his animosity towards Germans, evident in his inter-war writing, did not hesitate to step beyond his own shadow and show the power of genuinely committed art, which fights not for an ideology, however seductive, but for the human being.

Rajendra Chitnis (University of Bristol)
Jan Linka (Institute of Czech Literature,
Czech Academy of Science)

In his declining years, Václav Durych (b. 1930), manager of the estate of his late father, the present book's author Jaroslav Durych (1886–1962), and by 2001 very poorly himself, was (almost literally) dying to see *at least one* of his father's works translated into English; he was evidently unaware that *Bloudění* (Wandering, 1929) had appeared in an English translation by Lynton Hudson, as *The Descent of the Idol*, in London in 1935 and in New York a year later.[1]

Václav's promotional circular about his father's works (from which he explicitly excludes *Bloudění*, but only on the grounds of its bulk and the likely associated cost of any prospective translation, hence the assumption that he was unaware that it had been translated already) was forwarded to me by Renata Clark of Czech Centre London in November 2001. The immediate consequence was that I sat down

---

[1] That this translation has not been totally forgotten is attested by its inclusion in the late James Naughton's list of English translations from Czech literature, see http://babel.mml.ox.ac.uk/naughton/transl.html, used in particular by students of Czech and Slovak at Oxford and elsewhere in Britain.

and produced a specimen translation of the opening chapter of Durych's beautiful, unconventional love story *Sedmikráska* (Daisy). His son was thrilled with the translation, enthusing not least over my chosen title for the English version, *Bella* (perhaps only Czech- and English-speaking botanists will fully understand the motivation for the choice). And in January 2002, as a mark of his gratitude, he sent me the latest (2000) edition of *Sedmikráska* together with the third (1992) edition of his father's biography of St Adalbert (*Cesta svatého Vojtěcha*, first published in 1940). Incidentally, back in the 1930s, Karel Čapek (himself at the time the only widely translated Czech writer) and Czech PEN were in detailed negotiations with an American publisher to bring out a series of eight Czech novels deemed representative. Although he had been attacked by Durych quite violently in public in 1926, mockingly in the essay *Ejhle člověk!* (Ecce homo, 1928), and later in the essay *Pláč civilisty* (A Civilian's Lament, 1937), here for his lack of patriotism and his avoidance of military service, which Durych, himself an army doctor, thought downright immoral, it was Čapek who provided the list of suggested titles, including on it *Sedmikráska*.[2] It is surely unfortunate that nothing came of this project.

[2] I am indebted to my colleague Rajendra Chitnis for some of these details on the Čapek dimension.

My early encounter with translating Durych happened at a time when my full-time employment was all-consuming and the task went no further. I hadn't had a book-length translation published since 1983, and any further work on *Bella* – with no prospect of finding a publisher – eventually, and inevitably, fell back into second place behind work on Vítězslav Nezval's *Valerie and Her Week of Wonders*, for which there was a publisher and which duly appeared in 2005. So *Bella* never saw the light of day and it is now too late for Václav Durych, who died in November 2011, to appreciate that one (actually, one more) of his father's works – if not *Bella* – has, at last, appeared in English. From the afterlife of which both father and son had the deepest of Catholic convictions, may he perhaps look down now and rejoice.

The present translation was undoubtedly the toughest I have ever been asked to undertake (*Bella* had been no stroll in the park either). My first attempt to read the original in the early 1970s following its first, but posthumous, publication in 1969 ended in total failure: it was not an easy read, both because of the length of the somewhat mystifying Scottian (as I felt at the time) 'preamble' (and pre-amble) and because of the convoluted language, so heavily reliant on a high-style register with its often peripheral lexis, not to mention all the synaesthesia and paradoxes, or the complex similes and metaphors in the *Ich*'s mental meanderings. Had

I persevered, a third reason for failing to appreciate all that the book seeks to tell would undoubtedly have been my very ignorance of the historical and geopolitical background against which this story of the penitence, redemption and reconciliation of two of literature's more unusual protagonists unfolds (on which see the Afterword by Rajendra Chitnis and Jan Linka).

Since those days, however, I have felt rather better equipped to read and appreciate the book and even welcomed the invitation to undertake its translation, no matter how demanding the text. I believe that the nature of the source language – its lexical richness, its allusiveness, in part its rhythm and even its sporadic descents into a more colloquial vein – has broadly survived into the translation, but with what success it is for the reader to judge.

If there is one outstanding 'problem', it is the fact that the Czech word *had* means both 'snake' and 'serpent', so while the story gives an actual snake a hugely important role, I have managed to carry an echo of the 'serpent' sense only thrice and must hope that that will have sufficed to make the point – that we are in a kind of inverse Eden. Where the author chose to call the beast by its specific name, *zmije*, I have followed this consistently in the translation, though consciously choosing the more semantically laden 'viper' over its synonym 'adder'.

David Short, Windsor, 2016

In histories of Czech literature Jaroslav Durych (1886–1962) has been described as a 'Catholic writer'. This cliché says nothing about his poetics, merely indicating that he was one of the group of writers who, following the emergence of the Czechoslovak state in 1918, clung to the values of a church disesteemed by the young country. His early prose and verse is marked by an adherence to Symbolism and Parnassianism, but also to Catholic, notably Carmelite, mysticism. In a calculated manner he followed in the way of the allegorical, didactic prose of trashy nineteenth-century "novels for housemaids", though in his hands the writing is supremely poetic. In novels and short-stories of this type he extolled the beauty and poverty of young girls, qualities that become vehicles of the absolute (*Sedmikráska* [Bella, 1925], *Anežka Berková* [1931], *Duše a hvězda* [A Soul and a Star, 1969]). Most highly regarded is his historical prose, so clearly influenced by Expressionism and the language and motifs of the Baroque (*Bloudění* [1929, in English as *The Descent of the Idol*, 1935], *Rekviem* [Requiem, 1930], *Služebníci neužitečni* [Servants of the Lord to No Avail, 1969]). He also wrote very short stories and travel sketches with a highly distinctive conception of the role of narrator, while his essays on art can be quite arresting for their theoretical insights (*Váhy života a umění* [The Scales of Life and Art, 1933], *Rytmus české prózy* [The Rhythm of Czech Prose, 1992]). Durych was also a searing polemicist and ironic journalist (*Ejhle, člověk* [Ecce, Homo, 1928], and a poet of defiance, but also of utter devotion to the Virgin Mary (*Žebrácké písně* [Abject Hymns, 1926], *Té nejkrásnější* [To Her Who is Most Beautiful, 1929]). After World War II he wrote works that by and large could not be published until after his death (the family chronicle *Kouzelný kočár* [The Enchanted Carriage, 1995]).

Throughout, Durych advocates the transcendent values that, as he conceives them, protect man from the perils inherent in the modern way of life. He engaged in a war of words with such leading lights of the new Czechoslovakia as T. G. Masaryk and Karel Čapek, in whom he saw exponents of a superficial, pragmatic secularisation and ontological scepticism; in his celebration of poverty he was close to the political Left. His historical prose puts a dent in the superficial mythology of Czech ethnicity by elevating those ethical values that are universal.

ABOUT THE TRANSLATOR

David Short graduated with a BA in Russian and French from the University of Birmingham in 1965 and spent 1966–72 in Prague, studying Czech and linguistics, working, translating, having fun and eventually marrying a Czech fellow-student. He then taught Czech and Slovak at the School of Slavonic and East European Studies in London from 1973 to 2011. He has translated a wide range of literary and non-literary Czech texts, including several titles for Karolinum, and has won awards both for translations and for his contribution to Czech and Slovak studies, notably, in 2004, the Czech Minister of Culture's *Artis Bohemicae Amicis* medal and the Medal of the Comenius University in Bratislava.